A. C. Ramsey, Jean Strickland

The Autobiography of A.C. Ramsey

A. C. Ramsey, Jean Strickland

The Autobiography of A.C. Ramsey

ISBN/EAN: 9783337118198

Printed in Europe, USA, Canada, Australia, Japan

Cover: Foto ©Raphael Reischuk / pixelio.de

More available books at **www.hansebooks.com**

THE AUTOBIOGRAPHY
of
A. C. RAMSEY

SCHOOL TEACHER
and
CIRCUIT RIDER

EDITED BY
Jess Strickland

THE AUTOBIOGRAPHY OF A. C. RAMSEY

BY

A. C. RAMSEY

1879

Edited by

Jean Strickland
P. O. Box 5147
Moss Point, MS 39503

INTRODUCTION

The ensuing pages were copied from WPA Typescript of the Autobiography of Abner Clark Ramsey on file at the Department of
Archives and History, Montgomery, Alabama. No changes in spelling or
punctuation were made, since the typescript contains the notation
"copied from the original."

This is a first hand account of life in southeastern Mississippi
and southwest Alabama from 1809 to 1840 and was written by A. C.
Ramsey in 1879 from his first hand knowledge of the events as he lived
them. This manuscript was a primary source for Cyril Cain when he
was writing Four Centuries on the Pascagoula.

Much information of a genealogical nature is contained here in.
Since A. C. Ramsey was both a school teacher and Methodist Epicopal
Church Circuit Rider, he knew the families who lived in the area
personally. A first hand account of the first Camp Meeting at Salem
Camp Ground is especially interesting to Jackson Countians. The
location of many of the early churches in Mississippi and Alabama
can be pinpointed from this narrative.

After searching for several years to find the location of this
manuscript, it was finally located at the Archives in Montgomery,
Alabama. The Mississippi Archives did not have a copy. Nor did
any of the Universities contacted. This lack of availability to the
area it involves made me determined to make it available in printed
form for those it concerned.

The editing and annotating of this narrative was done in an
informal fashion because the narrative did not lend it self well to
formal footnotes. The writer had foot notes of his own on several
pages. Therefore periodically a page of Editor's Notes was added.
A serious effort was made to identify all Mississippi persons mentioned.
Place's were located and maps added. Sources of further information
were added also.

It is hoped that the reader will enjoy the narrative as well as
appreciate the vast amount of information within. It is truly an
insight into the past, into the day to day life of our ancestors who
braved the hardships to establish settlements in the pine country of
southeastern Mississippi and southwestern Alabama.

The Editor

A sketch

of the life and times of Rev. A. C. Ramsey as written by himself in
1879 at the age of 72.

together with a

short history of his Father and Mother and their descendants.

Connected with which

will be seen some allusions and incidents relating to the introduction,
rise and progress of the Methodist Episcopal Church and her pioneers
in South Eastern Mississippi from 1808 to 1832.

Gadsden Ala., September 1879

                              To

My children and their descendants
My borthers and sister's children and
descendants

            The following Biographical sketch

                         is

            Affectionately inscribed by

                              The Author

PREFACE

In compiling and writing up the following pages, I trust I have
been influenced by no other motive than a desire to preserve a record of
myself and family for the information and benefit of my children and relatives, when I am no more. And in doing this no attempt has been made at
fine style, or embellishment, even if the writer had have had the capacity
or his mind cultivated in that style it would have been avoided, in such
a history as is.here presented. Facts, and not their colouring is what has
been aimed at. His recollections, and other records have been called into
requisition, and taxed to their utmost capacity, in gleaning the most
prominent incidents and circumstances, connected with the subjects, and
history therein set forth. Imperfections no doubt exist, errors especially
in dates, may be apparent but the incidents and facts, are true, although
his recollection of the exact year or time of their occurance may have been
at fault. But believing it imbodies, in the main as correct a statement,
of a family, noted only for honesty, integrity, respectability and may I
add piety as could but had I send it forth praying God's blessings upon
it.

The Author

Editor's Note:

From Passports of Southeastern Pioneers 1170 - 1823 by Dorothy Williams
Porter (Baltimore, MD: Gateway Press, Inc., 1982).

Georgia Executive Proceedings ... February 1808 - November 1809, page
413; drawer 50, roll 46.

Executive Department
Wednesday 26th April 1809

On the recommendation of several respectable inhabitants of the
State of South Carolina

Ordered

That a passport be prepared for William Ramsay through the Creek
Nation

Which was presented and signed

I was born in Jackson County, Georgia, November 4th 1807. My father William Ramsey was born in Mecklenburg County, North Carolina July 27th, 1770. My mother whose maiden name was Elizabeth Huey, was born in Ireland September 15th, 1787. Her parents, Andrew and Nancy Huey, came to America when she was an infant and settled in Pennsylvania. How long they remained in that State I do not know; but moved from there to Georgia, and settled in Franklin County; if my memory is correct. And here let me remark that this with many others narrated in this sketch, are given from recollections of what my parents told me, many long years ago. My father was twice married his first wife was a Miss Woodside, who lived but a short wile after their marriage, and left no issue. And whether their marriage took place in North Carolina or Georgia I am not prepared to state positively, but think it was in the former state. Father moved to Georgia, but at what time I do not know. He thus became acquainted with Mother, and at a proper time married her. They settled in Jackson County, to which Grandfather Huey had moved. Here my borther Andrew and myself were born; the only two out of the five who were native Georgians.

In the fall of 1807 or thereabouts, Father hearing that a fine country was ahead and that it was to be found in the New Territory, that the United States had just acquired from the Choctaw Indians, in what is now south-eastern Mississippi, and a part of which is included in what is now Wayne, Greene, Jackson, Hancock and Harrison Counties; determined to move to it; so as soon as he could arrange for the trip, packed up and started. This was I presume in the early part of 1808, when I was but a few months old. I think sometimes in January of that year.

- His Outfit and Conveyance -

This consisted of three horses; upon two of which he packed his bedding, clothing, camp equipage and c as much as the strength of his locomotives could bear. The other horse was appropriated, to Mother's use, to convey her; brother Andrew, and myself, to the land of promise. Upon this horse she rode, carrying me before, and brother behind her the entire trip; while Father and the Negro girl Dinah walked, and managed the pack horses.

- The Perils of the Trip -

Having to pass nearly the entire way through an Indian Country (now Alabama) were often and almost constantly exposed to depredations and dangers from

Editors note:

Record Group 5, Legislative Records, Territorial Archives, Volume 26,
Petitions of the General Assembly, 1804 - 1809, Mississippi Department
of Archives and History, Jackson, MS

PETITION

To the Honorable: The Legislative Council and House of Representatives
of the Mississippi Territory.

   The petition of the undersigned inhabitants of Washington County,
living on the Chickasawhay River humbly sheweth that the nearest part of
the Chickasawhay settlement is distant from the Courthouse upwards of
forty miles and the extreme parts upwards of sixty that a number of us
are compelled to attend court twice in every year three weeks at a time
at considerable expence to ourselves and the loss frequently of our crops.
As a number of us are men who have families depending alone on our labor
for a support, that from the situation of the country it is sometimes next
to impossible for those of us who have suits depending in Court to get
there on account of high watters whereby great injustice may be done the
parties. Your petitioners represent that the Chickesawhay settlement
at present near forty miles in length and that is upwards of sixty miles
from the huwannee Town on the Chickasawhay river to where the Spanish
line crosses the same & we humbly conceive that there is already a sufficient number of inhabitants on the Chickesawhay River to entitle them to
a county and the population fast increasing by emigrants from other parts
of the United States.
   Your petitioners therefore humbly pray that your honorable body
will take their case into consideration and have them a county laid off
on 'he Chickesawhay River and your petitioners are in duty bound will
ever pray & c.
December 16, 1808

James Patton	Tisdall Whatley	James Bilbo
Arthur Patton	Jno Pike	Richard Nye
William Ramsey	John Philips	Jacob Neely
Daniel Huey	Iham B. Philips	Joseph Neely
Thos. Sumrall	Chas. Heaton	Thos Neely
John Lanier	Mick. Ehlert	David Kelly
Alexander McIntosh	George Dickey	Jas. Neely
Joseph Patton	George Johnston	Jacob Newton
Henry Snelgrove	John McGaughey	Jurden Margen
Jas. Griffen	William Williams, Senr.	Hardey Woten
James Morgan	Herrin Williams	Burrel Posey
Elisha Morgan	Benjamin Williams	Stephen Correll
Elijah Morgan	William Williams	William Hammelton
Thomas Morgan	James Taylor	Sampson Mounger
Simeon Williams	Samuel Newton	Harris Mounger
Josiah Skinner	John Williams	William Webber
John Evins	John Lott	Joseph Jones
Edward Gatlin	Jesse Lott	John Barwen
Mathew Dickerson	Luke Lott	John Brewer, Sen.
Wyche Watley	Robert Lott	MS Illegible
Amos Reed	James Thomas	John Young
Luke Patrick	Micajah Wall	MS illegible
____Dupree	Daniel Whitehead	James Proctor

Jourdan Proctor	John Munger	R. B. George
John Gordan	David Horn	Giles Sumril
Calvin Sumril	Wood_____MS illegible	

Franklin County,Georgia Tax List 1798
(From: Franklin County, Georgia Tax Digests, Volume I - 1798-1807
by Martha Walters Acker, page 10 and 128).

William Ramsy - 287½ acres value $576.00   1798 Tax Roll

Andrew Hughey - 1 negro; 287½ acres bounded by David Leak, Wm Haley
and Indian Creek; 200 acres, bounded by David Leak, Few and Sandy
Creek(Jackson County).   1803 Tax Roll

The above are probably the grandparents of A. C. Ramsey. The 1809
Georgia passport and the 1808 petition of citizens of the Mississippi
Territory would appear to make it unclear as to when William Ramsey
arrived in the Mississippi Territory. However, it is likely that
the petition was begun in 1808 and not presented to the legislature
until 1809. During the December 1809 session of the Legislature of
the Territory, Wayne County was created.

The 1810 and 1811 Tax Rolls of Wayne County, Mississippi Territory
show the following:

William Ramsey - 1 white poll; 1 slave; Tax 1.75

the savage tribes, yet strange to think they were the most of the way treated kindly at least friendly; with some few exceptions. Another difficulty
met them frequently at different points on their route: swollen creeks
and rivers often retarded their headway; and having to make their way
through, following Indian trails, no roads, ferries or bridges (as now)
were frequently dependant upon the Indians for aid, and the use of small
skiffs, or rather dugouts, in making the crossings over many streams which
they encountered.

But they finally reached their destination, and settled down on the
Chickasawha River, near or at the line, then dividing the Choctaw Nation,
(as it was called) from the newly acquired territory of the United States;
and the place is near if not at, the present location of the town of
Waynesborough in Wayne County, Mississippi. They arrived here on the
21st day of February 1808. Their estate consisted now, of the three horses,
what baggage they had brought, the negro girl Dinah and twenty-one (21.00)
dollars in cash.

Now as might be supposed; discouragements of a trying character met
them; being late in the season, a cabin to build, land to clear, provisions
to look after, very little to be had near them, but a few neighbors and
those, like themselves, new comers; no corn nearer than St. Stephens on the
Bigby River, forty or fifty miles distant; and when obtained there cost four
dollars per bushel; and requiring several days travel to get it and having
such small capital upon which to depend, and provisions of all kinds, being
in proportion to corn. We may well imagine these difficulties could but
produce sadness and discouragements; so much so they often wished themselves back in Georgia. These were emphatically, in the strict and true
sense of the term "Hard Times" about which the present generation know but
little. And it may be presumed, yea reduced to a centily that the luxuries
of living were not and could not be indulged. Bread and meat, milk and
butter, were the constant bill of fare, even among those who could obtain
them. Yet none of us perished, we struggled through. But how could we at
the present day get along under such disadvantages; many failing hearts I
fear would be the result.

Father erected a cabin as soon as he could; put us in it, and commenced
preparations for a farm.

- Mode of clearing and planting -

4

This consisted in cutting down the cane in the swamp with a cane hoe or hatchet, which he procured in some way, letting it lie on the ground until dry, then burning it off; and such was the efficiency of this mode, that the burning did not only consume the dry cane, but a great portion of the timber and debris on the ground, would also burn up, so that the clearing would be in good order for planting; besides much of the green timber was deadened by the intense heat. The planting was done by making holes at proper distances, depositing the seed covering with the same earth taken out in making the hole. No fences nor plowing necessary, all that is needed was to keep down the mutton cane, butter weeds &c with the hoe.

But this preparation required time and labour, so that on the 4th day of July Father finished planting his corn and pumpkins. Such was the richness and character of this loam soil at that time that it required a short time for corn to mature; early killing frosts were also uncommon, so that although father was late getting his in the ground, yet in gathering it in the fall, he not only made a plenty for home consumption but a surplus for market, and as to his pumpkin crop I recollect distinctly to have heard him say repeatedly that he "could nearly walk all over his field stepping on pumpkins".

– Other Labours Performed –

During this period, he had to provid means and facilities for clothing the family as well as feeding them. Consequently he obtained in some way a spinning wheel. My recollection is, it was made by one of his neighbors, old Mr. Rodgers, who I think worked at the business of chair and wheel making. Father made some of his own chairs, which lasted us in the family for a number of years. He also got a pair of cotton cards; and then made a loom, on the Georgia style and called the Georgia loom, I believe to this day. This was made by placing two pieces of timber, generally a log of the right size split into two halves at the side of the base, as the receiver of thread cloth and breast beams, and an additional arrangement above for harness, batton, stay &c. The machine was complete and ready for operating. This rough structure formed in those times, and long after, the "modus operandi" of manufacturing all such goods and clothing as were worn by males and females. These manufacturing implements being furnished, it was next in order to put them to work. Accordingly Mother being the operator, went to work. First bought the cotton in the seed and had to pay for it in spinning or weaving. The cotton had to be picked by hand, with the

fingers which was generally done at night, by the whole family, old and
young. Subsequently, however, some improvement was made in this direction
of what was called the hand gin, which required two hands to operate it; so
that some nights, ginned cotton would be obtained sufficient to run the wheel
the next day. This little simple machine, was generally operated by the
smaller or younger members of the family. And O it makes me sad to think
now, of the many unpleasant nights I have passed, astride the bench turning the squeaking rollers; I nodding; and the pile of seed cotton getting
no smaller. Mother sometimes scolding us a little, and at others cheering
us up; the task must be finished. All this was not only annoying, but often have I wished the old gin in the fire, but such was life then.

With these facilities, rough and unhandy as they were, Mother not
only clothed the family, but made a surplus for market, which Father in
the fall of that year carried to Mobile and sold for $2.50 per yard. Mobile
was then under Spanish control and country produce or manufactures very
high.

- Their Misfortunes -

During that year the Indians stole one of their horses, a second one
fell off the river bluff and was drowned, the third one Father had sold for
cattle, but whether all this occured that year 1808 or the next I do not
remember distinctly, but think the sale of the one was the first year and
the losses the second. This was to them a sad misfortune. And the question
now would naturally arise how did they manage to live and get along, with
these disadvantages, mishaps and misfortunes and such a small capital to
operate on? Well, I do not know; but "where there is a will, there is a
way" and by constant, unceasing industry, and economy close saving, hard
living, frugality, and care, and with it all an abiding trust in, and firm
reliance upon the Providence of God, they were sustained and lived independent of debt.

With this unpromising commencement at their new home; they managed to
live, and accumulate some little means, and gather together those and
afterwards some little stock, by attention to which and its increase connected with their energy and correct habits of life, they were enabled to raise
their children, five in number, in credit and respectability, bestowing upon
them all such intellectual culture and education, as their means and the
facilities of the country would justify. But above all "training of them

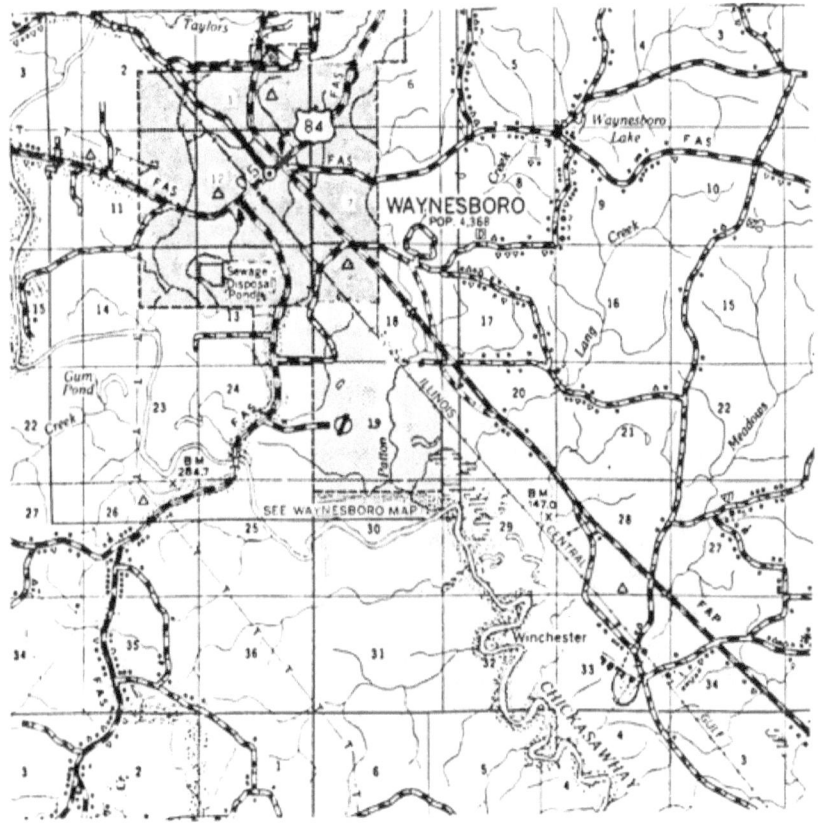

Section 30, Township 8, Range 6W is probable location of the Ramsey home
when they lived near the present site of Waynesboro, MS. Old Mr. Rodgers
referred to on page 5 is probably Joseph Rodgers who is referred to in
the land records as residing in Township 8, Range 6W. No land is shown
for William Ramsey in the St. Stephens Land Office Records in Wayne County.
This would not be unusual since the land in Wayne County had not yet
been offered for sale in 1809 and 1810.

up in the way they should go" and fixing in their minds while young such convictions and lessons of moral truth and piety, that led them to "Remember their Creator in the days of their youth."

The aim and object of this parental training was to fix in the young minds, such correct principles, as would lead to the adoption and culti- vation of all those rules of moral and religious experience and practice as would secure them against the evil tendencies of depraved nature, and the corruptions of evil society, and thereby be developed in an honorable stand in this to a useful citizenship among men and worthy and useful members of the church of God.

And in this I am rejoiced to note, their labours, objects and aims were not altogether in vain although this may have been in some instances the fruits of true Christian piety in all its phases and degrees; they shown and developed in a correct life of moral deportment and integrity.

- Indian Annoyances -

During this year they were often much annoyed with the Indians. Although no violence was ever attempted by them. But living as they did immediately on the trail leading from the "Six Towns" in the nation to Mobile which was their market, going there sometimes in great crowds, and making it a point generally to camp near the houses of the white settlers, especially on their return home; and bringing great loads of whickey; and caring but little for anything else in their purchases at market, but powder, lead and whiskey, a good supply of the latter was generally laid in, and conveyed in kegs and as a consequence fighting, scratching, and yelling was generally kept up as long as the whickey held out. And that greatly to the annoyance and confusion of the whites around and about their campfires at which they would stay several days and nights. They had a system however, in their drunken sprees. One would remain sober to protect and keep the drunken ones out of the fire, and prevent them from killing each other in their fights, and do police duty in general, whose duty also required him to keep them from interrupting the white people, especially the ladies.

Hence Mother at first was considerably alarmed, but was told by the sober sentinels "not to be uneasy, they should not hurt her". And so it proved no violence or insults allowed to be offered. They alternated in doing guard duty, the one watch to day would take his turn drinking tomorrow and one of the drunken ones today would take his place and so on.

- Their Moves From Now On -

At the close of this year 1808 Father sold his place and moved further
down the river. He appeared to take up the idea, that improving new places
and selling them out, to other new comers (and there were many) was better
for him; more money in it; than to remain at one place and make larger improvements and thereby accumulate money sufficient to buy or enter him a permanent
home, when these government lands were put into market which he anticipated
would be at no very distant day, which was even so. But I think it this he
realized his mistake.

He now settled the place where Winchester, the county site of Wayne
County now is situated, (or if not now was the county site, originally).
He cut the first stick of timber, felled the first tree there, and made the
first improvements where that town now stands. Here he made improvements
like unto his former one, made one or two crops, and sold out; again this
was in 1809. He may have lived at this place two years and probably did;
here my recollection is at fault, but think possibly he remained at this
place 1810 as in this year my sister Ann was born and I think at this place.

He afterwards lived in the neighborhood of the Patton's, Poes, and
Webber, but at what particular place I have no means of determining, but
that he remained in that vicinity, I mean, Winchester and the country contiguous to it, three years 1809 - 1811 for brother William was born in that
region in the latter part of 1811. The conviction on my mind is, after he
left the Winchester place he lived in 1811 near Mother Patton's. One circumstance occured at her home which confirms me in this belief. Father and
Mother spent a night there on a visit I suppose; it was a very cold night,
heavy frost on the ground; I was then I suppose four years old, probably less.
My mother called my attention to a flock of geese in the yard, where I saw
one standing on one foot holding up the other. This struck me so forcibly,
I have never forgotten it. That with the appearance of Mother Patton one
of the first things I remember in this world, and it must have been in the
winter of 1810 or at farthest 1811.

I think Father made a mistake on moving so often; clearing, improving
so many new places subjecting him to such severe exposure and hard labour,
which no doubt contributed greatly in laying the foundation of the disease
which finally terminated his life. Besides this the country was then new
and lands fertile; the range for stock good; bottom or river lands covered
with solid cane breaks, easy to clear, water and health good; and looking

9

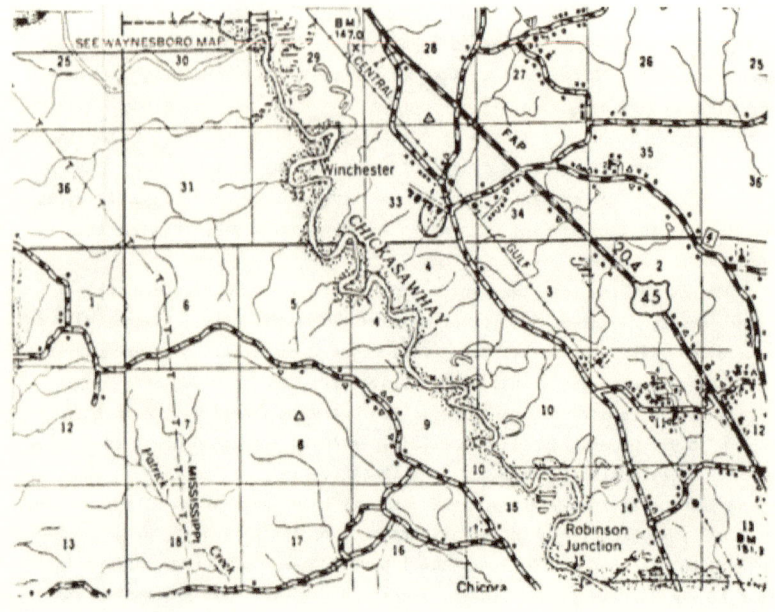

Editors Note:

Above map shows location of Winchester and area of location of William
Ramsey after his first move. The families of Patton, Powe (Poes) and
Webber that are spoken of are probably James Patton, William and
Alexander Powe and William Webber. Patton's fort is located in this
area, as well as the old James Patton Home. James Patton's grave is
in the woods back of the old Patton Home; he was born in SC 1735 and died
in Wayne County, MS in 1813. The William Powe and Alexander Powe cemeteries
are also in this area, Section 10 and 25, Township 7, Range 6 Wayne County.
William Powe and his wife Elizabeth Pegues Powe are buried in the William
Powe cemetery and Alexander Powe and his wife, Elizabeth Spencer Powe
are buried in the Alexander Powe cemetery.

back now from the present standpoint, it appears that could he have been
contented to have remained there permanently with his energy and economy
he might have done well. But he thought differently and so acted and
probably all for the best.

- Their Church Privileges -

These were ordinary. In 1808 a missionary of the M. E. Church
was sent into that country by the name of "Sturdivant" who preached for
them occasionally; and in 1809 the same one in connection with "Michael
Bur~e", travelled through that country on what was then called "Tombeckbee
Mission", a large Mission, embracing a large territory of country, on and
between, and contiguous to, the Alabama, Tombechbee and Chickasawha Rivers;
stretching southward near the coast. Whether a society was formed there
either of those years, of which they became a member, I am not certain, but
think there was. As I remember to have heard them say they were members
when Father Burger (as they called him) was with them; and often related
some quaint and amusing anecdote of the good old brother and at whose house
their's was his stopping place when in that part of the mission. I recollect
also hearing them speak of being associated in the church with Father Webber,
Mrs. Patton and others in that community.

- Their Religious Training -

They were both brought up and raised strict Presbyterians particularly
Father, whose Father was of the strictest and straightest sect. So much so,
that when there was a split in that church on the subject of Psalmody and
causing the organization of that branch known as "Seceders", Grandfather
Ramsey adhered to them and was so opposed to the use of Dr. Watts' version
of the Psalms, except Rouse's, I heard Father say that he threatened to
burn Watts' if it was brought into his house. But I believe he finally gave
up those notions and affiliated with the Presbyterians.* My mothers parents
were of the same faith and order, but not as strenious as Grandfather Ramsey.

My impression is they both[X] united with the Methodist Church before
they left Georgia, and brought with them their certificates of membership
to their new home.

---

* Grandfather Ramsey's ancestors were from Scotland, and belonged to the
old Covenanters and of course his religious training was in that school of
Calvinistic Theogoly.

X Father and Mother

Editor's Notes:

Sturdivant referred to on page 10 is Matthew P. Sturdivant, probably the first minister to visit the Tombigbee settlement, other than the famed evangelist Lorenzo Dow. Dow referred to the people of the Tombigbee settlement as being very wicked and worldly and not in the least interested in religion. Michael Burge joined Matthew P. Sturdivant in the Tombigbee and Chickasawhay area for a time.

History of Methodism in Mississippi by John G. Jones

Editor is unable to identify "Father Burger" on page 10. Possibly it is meant to Burge and may be Burge in the original handwriting of the author. The Editor is working from a typescript copy made by the W.P.A. and filed in the Alabama Department of Archives and History, Montgomery, AL.

Mrs. Patton, page 10, is Mrs. James Patton.

Father Webber, page 10, is William Webber.

"In 1809, Sturdevant and Burdge had a preaching place and organized a Society on the Chickasahay in the neighborhood of the present town of Winchester, eight or ten miles west of the present line of Alabama. A Mr. Webber, a Mrs. Patton, William Ramsey and his wife Elizabeth were original members of this Society. There is at this date, no information as to who besides these, if any, belonged to that Society at its organization."

History of Methodism in Alabama by Lazenby

But whether or not they did so very soon after their arrival there
for I have no recollections of ever hearing or knowing them to be anything
else but Methodist and invariably leading spirits in that denomination.

And even if they had been disposed to have adhered to the church in
which they had been brought up, there was no chance for them in that new
country to have affiliated with it. No Presbyterian preacher or missionary
had found his way into this desert waste as yet; and consequently no church
of that order.

But I wish to record it here to their credit, and the credit of that
large intelligent and Christian denomination, that the lessons taught them
and impressions made upon their minds in early life together with a sense
of the moral obligations upon them in the strict observance of the command-
ments of God stuck to them and was seen and exemplified in their lives and
habits through life and in training their children. The vigilance and care
exercised over them and particularly was this manifest in the observance of
the sanctity of the holy Sabbath.

— Their Next Move —

Father's next move was to Greene County. I think in the early part of
1812, to the neighborhood of "Bethel Church" near where the present county
site of Greene County is now situated, known as Leakesville. Here he was
associated with a community of excellent citizens, such as John McRai,
William Martin, Norman McDuffee, Roderick McDuffee, Alexander McIntosh,
Daniel McIntosh, McInnis, McLeods, Smith and others. The most of whom were
Scotch from North Carolina, and had built them a church and united with the
Methodist Church, and were served once every four weeks, by the itinerant
preachers of that denomination who were then according to the law of the
church changed every year. Father John McRae was a leading and zealous
spirit in that church occupying the position of class leader and with whom
my father was soon associated in the same office; who held their meetings
every Sabbath; and to which all the members were expected and required to
attend. And it was an established custom that parents were not only expected there, attending upon this special means of grace, but the children
had to go also.

Well do I remember (although quite young, the shouts, songs, prayers,
and exortations and happy seasons of these occasions. At that time mysterious to my young mind, but fully understood and appreciated now. Another
feature in those meetings of early Methodist usages was the class was regularly examined by the leader in regard to their religious experience,

13

life and trials; and even the little boys and girls, who were required to
stay in class (as it was called) would receive at the hand of the "sub-
shepherds of the flock, a word of advice and counsel with a pat on the head,
and "be a good boy or girl and learn to read the Bible and say your prayers
&c. This old brother McRae was not only a leading man in the church, but
in the community generally whose opinions and judgement were much respected,
whose kindness and hospitality was invariably extended to the needy and
suffering. The people of that part of the Territory honored him, by
electing him a member to the Convention that formed that Territory into
a State. The State of Mississippi. Note: Attendance upon class meetings
was at that time and for many years afterwards, a test of membership. Non
attendance for so many successive meetings forfeited connection with the
church. Not so now, although it still forms a part of Methodist usage and
economy that feature has been removed. Hence attendance upon these meetings
is discretionary and not compulsory. A wise improvement, in the opinion of
this writer.

- His First Settlement in This Community -

was on rented land, immediately on the bluff of the Chickasawha River
where there was a ferry about one mile from Father McRae's and Bethel Church.
This was a very sickly year, and a sickly place. Here our family were all
stricken down with fever and ague, so that often one was not able to give
another a drink of water. By the kind hospitality of Father McRae we were
all taken to his house and cared for until we recovered. Father did not
remain at that place, but this one year(and I am not certain, but think he
did not go back there after our severe spell of sickness) in consequence of
the exposure continually to the feverish Miazma of the river and swamp. Two
other incidents occured there which also added much to the dislike of the
place, which proved to him the constant danger of some of us getting drowned.
The first was in my own case. One one occasion while the negro woman Dinah
was washing at the river's edge, at the ferry, where lay the ferry boat, or
flat which was in fifty yards I suppose of the house, on the bluff. I was
there playing in the flat, which lay broad side or parallel, with the bluff
or bank. A skiff or batteau lying between the flat and the bank, in very
close proximity to the side of the flat, and being desirous to get into the
skiff, commenced the operation, by clenching the gunnels of the flat with
both hands, put my feet into the skiff, which pushed it off from the side
of the flat. Trying to retain my foot hold on the skiff, let loose my hold
on the flat and under the flat I went head formost. And that would have been

14

the last of me, but for the timely aid of Aunt Dinah, who waded in reached
under the flat and fortunately caught my foot and pulled me out. She gave
the alarm. Mother came and the first thing I remembered was she had me lying
with my head downwards and water running out at my mouth. Thus was I saved.
And I have always attributed the safety of my life to Aunt Dinah's vigilence
and presence of mind at that time. The other incident, occured with brother
William who was then crawling. The bluff of the river, not being more than
twenty yards, I suppose, from the door of the house, which was steep and
perpendicular and the river swollen. And he having escaped Mother's vigil-
ent watch over him, crawled out at the door and made his way to the bluff,
where he perched himself, with his feet hanging over the edge of the preci-
pice enjoying himself looking at the deep waters below. In this condition,
Mother happened to see him, and having presence of mind enough not to speak
or make any noise which would doubtless have caused him to move or slip off,
she slipped up quietly behind him, picked him up, and thus saved him from
a watery grave. These two circumstances caused him to determine, in connection with the sickness of the place, that he would seek a less dangerous place.
Accordingly he secured a place near William Martins in the same neighborhood.
On this place he lived in 1813.

- The Indian War -

was now raging at a fearful rate. During this year the first battle with
the Creeks, or Muskogee Indians was fought on Burnt Corn Creek in Conecuh
County, Alabama sometime in the 3pring of that year; and subsequently the
fall and massacre of Fort Mims occured the same year, August 30. The news
reached our neighborhood where we lived of the fall of this fort and its
horrid results, and that the savages in large file were marching westward;
and had killed several person in the fork of Bigby and Alabama Rivers near
Fort Sinquefield,* and were marching on that settlement on the Chickasawha
River, and would probably be there by the next morning; — the last part of
this report proved untrue, the massacre and killing were facts as reported.
I well remember the afternoon when this news reached us - the alarm; the
horror and consternation it produced. The men were mostly in their fields
at work; — the women running to and fro, hither and thither; blowing horns,
sending runners &c for the men, not knowing what to do, where to go, and
how to evade the fate they then saw before them. But finally the men were
assembled, a council held; and a decision arrived at; which was to pack

* now called Fort Adams

15

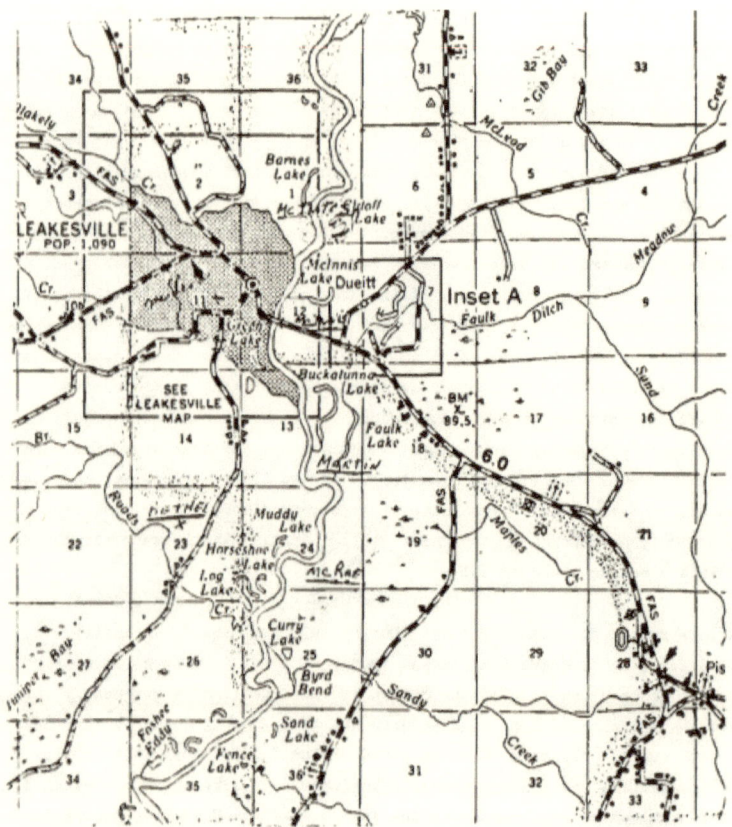

Editor's Note:
The above map shows approximate location of Bethel Meeting House. The
History of Methodism in Alabama by Lazenby locates it as two miles west
of the Chickasawhay River and about two miles below the present town of
Leakesville. This would locate it approximately in Section 23.
Daniel McIntosh lived in Section, Township 2 North, Range 6 West.
John McInnis lived in Section 12, Township 2 North, Range 6 West. Accord-
ing to Claiborne in his Trip through the Piney Woods, McInnis kept an
inn of sorts in Leakesville on the banks of the Chickasawhay where the
court met.
Daniel Martin lived in Section 13, Township 2 North, Range 6West.
John McRae lived in Section 24, Township 2 North, Range 6 West.
Records of St. Stephens, M.T. Land Office, Special Collections, Gorgas
Library, University of Alabama indicate the above land owners.

16

up and hide all their goods and chattels in the swamps except such as they could take with them and leave the neighborhood, and go to any place where they might suppose at least they would be safe from the merciless hand of the destroyer.

This order was promptly obeyed; and such packing, and lugging off to the swamp (some quarter of mile from our place) had never been seen in that country before. But finally all things were adjusted; those who had wagons called them into requisition; those who had ferry boats got into them; such as had horses saddled them, and such as had neither took it a foot. And a general stampede made some down the river in their boats; some to the river swamps, some to a pine woods and so on; mostly to the pine woods and back settlements, however. Father's conveyance consisted of two horses. On one, Mother, William and I were seated; Willie in her lap, and I behind. On the other Father with sister Ann before him, brother Andrew behind, Dinah the negro girl a foot. On we went in the company with several others, it being now dark, but fortunately the moon shined brightly; and after a tiresome ride (to me at least) of about five or six miles through the pine woods, we rounded to and tied up at Aunt Nepsey McRae's, a sister of Father John McRae's. Here we passed the night, I do not know how comfortable to the grown people, but to me it was as calm as if there had not been an Indian in a thousand miles of us. Suppose I slept so sound I never once thought of an Indian.

The next morning the men of the party went back to see what had been done, and ascertain the result, when to their gratification were informed "it was a flase alarm" that the Indians were not advancing on us. It turned out some badly scared fellow having heard of their depredations at Fort Mims and Fort Sinquefield, supposed they were coming on and passed through the country and so reported it as a fact.

If he had been found there the next day I think some of the men would have made him wished he had never heard of an Indian. All hands returned home; goods and chattles gathered up and peace restored. These incidents that I am relating are nearly as fresh in my memory now at age of 72 as when they transpired. In fact my recollection of things then is more acute and vivid than a few years back. One other incident occured here which made that year a memorable one to me. There lived on or near this place a man by the name of Carson, a blacksmith and I believe a gunsmith, whose shop was directly on the road between Father's house and Mr. Martins. It so

17

happened I was at Mr. Martins one afternoon playing with his little boys,
and Carson was at his shop in company of another man, working on a gun, and
very soon commenced shooting at a mark. I being very fearful of a gun
(and am until yet) the report of which alarmed and frightened me dreadfully;
commenced crying and screaming and tried to run home (which was a short
distance) but Carson was in my way. I could not get by him as I thought,
without being shot, and here I was Mrs. Martin trying to pacify me, but
failing Carson pointed the gun at me and snapped it; this almost threw me
into fits, of course the gun was not loaded, but I did not know any differ-
ence then in a loaded gun and an empty one, a gun was a gun with me, and had
naturally a dread of them.

Finally he stopped, I passed him and ran home screaming at the top of
my voice. Father met me, "what is the matter," he asked. My reply was
"Mr. Carson shot me". He examined me but found no wounds, but was very
much excited at this man's conduct, and went over immediately and gave
him a piece of his mind, for alarming me so badly and not trying to allay
my excitement.

- His Next Move -

was to a place on the east side of the river near Samuel Warren's who
had a ferry. Here he remained one year 1814 and at this place and in
this year brother Daniel was born.

There are two or three incidents, connected with this place as occuring
that year that I must relate in addition to the one above. And first,
Father's house was as long as I can remember, a stopping place and resting
place for the preachers who would often hold what was called night meetings
at the private houses, and often at his house. That year Thomas Owens was
on that circuit, who preached regularly at the Church, Bethel, on the opposite side of the river, but for some cause, I do not know what; I suppose
for convenience to the neighbors around and wishes of Father and Mother; he
had an appointment at Fathers at night. A respectable congregation present,
during services, I fell asleep while sitting on the edge of the bed, and
making a long nod pitched forward on the floor and skinned my nose, producing some little stir in the congregation of course. But after service
closed and in fixing a bed for the preacher, who was a little choice, insisted on Mother putting his bed on the floor before the fire. And let it be
remembered houses were not roomy and capacious then as now, not many rooms;

and but two to this of ours; and in one of them the Misses McRae, Margaret
and Jane, who tarried there that night, occupied, so that the preacher had
to stop in the room with the old folks and children, where a good comfortable bed was prepared and set apart for him, but no, he did not want to
sleep on a bed only before the fire — accordingly he was accommodated.
During the night, a wind arose and a heavy blast swept down the chimney,
carrying with it quantities of soot that had accumulated, and blowing it
all over th preacher and his bed; but did not arouse him. He lay unconscious
of it until after day light when father laughing in his sleeve awoke him,
told him to "get up and look in the glass". He had rolled about in it
until not only his clothes but face and hands were almost black. I thought
that morning I saw a preacher a little mad, and what added to it, was while
he was out with soap and water, scrubbing and washing the two young ladies
came out, and laughed so heartily at him he could hardly keep his temper.
He washed up however and got over it. And considered this possibly as one
of the felicities of itinerancy in a new country.

Another mishap befell me at that place. The last whipping Father ever
gave me was here this year, and for no other reason than like poor "Tray"
for being in bad company. A man by the name of Hays lived on the place that
year, and I think he made a crop with Father, had two sons Charles and
William, whose size and ages corresponded with that of brother Andrew's and
mine, hence playmates to each of us. A public road ran near the house, we
were, one morning, all out playing not very far from the road; Charlie and
Andrew, together, and William and I off some distance from them; when it
happened a lady, or a woman at least, passed down the road with a large
bundle of cabbage or greens of some kind on her head. Charley and Andrew,
very impertenantly commenced hallowing at her "Good morning to your night
cap" and repeated it two or three times, which very much insulted her. She
went to the house and told our Fathers; here they came, with hickory in hand,
each of them and let in and dressed us all. William and I were perfectly
innocent, and I thought then and told Father afterwards after I grew up that
he ought to have discriminated between the guilty and innocent; yet it learned me a lesson; never to insult a woman, even in fun. But that woman who
by the by was a single woman, and I believe an old maid at that; had many
bad wishes and prayers heaped on her that morning by us; one was that she
might marry a man that would give her the hickory and abuse her badly, and
I think I heard these prayers were answered.

19

Editor's Note:

page 17 - "A man by the name of Carson, a blacksmith ..". Editor cannot
identify this man. He does not appear on the tax list for Greene County,
MS for the period 1810 - 1820.

Page 18 - Samuel Warren was from Georgia;born about 1779 in Liberty
County, Georgia; married Elizabeth Harrell also of Georgia. They were
possessed of considerable estate. Samuel Warren was dead by 1819 when
the Tax Rolls show John McRae as administrator of his estate. The
widow Elizabeth Harrell Warren married second, in Greene County, MS
John Pritchard.

Page 18 - Thomas Owens - History of Methodism in Alabama by Lazenby
Rev. Thomas Owens was the junior preacher on the Tombigbee Charge in
1815, and then again in 1818. He was born in South Carolina, January
8, 1787. When but a child he went with his parents to the Natchez country,
where he grew to manhood. When this incident occurred, he was about
twenty eight years old and an unmarried man.

Page 19. A man named Hays - Editor is unable to identify this man.
There are no men named Hays on the tax rolls for Greene County, MS
for the period 1810 - 1820.

During this year, the struggle with the Indians terminated for that
time. Gen. Jackson and his coadjutors had whipped them into a treaty of
peace. An account of this sanguinary war can fully be seen in "Brewer's
History of Alabama" and also in "Picketts". A treaty of peace was concluded and signed 9th August 1814 by the leading chiefs and warriors. (Brewer)

This closed the war on the Tallapoosa; but dissatisfaction existed
with a large portion of the tribe, against those who had signed this treaty,
and they fled to Pensacola, and were protected by the Spaniards; and became
warriors under them. Mobile had been taken from the Spaniards which much
incensed them and they arranged to recapture it and commenced the campaign.
But the American troops under Gen. Jackson repulsed them on their first
attempt, and not only held Mobile, but marched on Pensacola. Where Gen.
Jackson captured it and its defenses Nov. 7th. So ended the sanguinary
Indian War, "called the Creek War" and a final settlement and adjustment
entered into and consumated and peace restored.

The Choctaw Indians were a friendly tribe, and even assisted the whites
in this contest against the Creeks. And after the close of the war of the
Tallapoosa, they considered the whites under great obligations to them,
for having assisted them, in whipping the Creeks; and on returning home
from the war, would invariably call on the white settlers, to feed them
or contribute such things to them, as they, saw about the premises to which
they took a fancy. They were a lazy tribe; and other tribes, for instance,
the Creeks "said they were "cowards". Hence the reason of their friendship
to the whites. But be this as it may, they rendered valuable service in
the struggle at several engagements, and different occasions, which was
I think accorded to them and appreciated by the whites.

I recollect distinctly during that year, after the close of the war,
crowds of them passing Fathers and invariably begging on the plea to
which I have already alluded. Their way of asking was — Sup-pe-ta:
Bob a Sheila, check a maw fawa which was - - Give me some; we are friends -
"good excellent". Hence if they wanted milk, it was - Pish ic; sup-pe-ta;
if corn, Ton-sha Sup-pe-ta; if bread Bus-pa sup-pe-ta; and so on. They
generally carried along a scalp taken from an Indian's head, and stretched
and dried on the top of a staff; as a trophy of their valor in the war.
Having also a tin cup covered tightly with deer skin which they used as
a drum; and wind up their visits with a war dance in which all engaged,
squaws, and men; forming a ring. One man sitting in the center beating

this little drum, and other in the circle carrying the scalp as their flag. Here they would go around and round, stopping at a certain time of the dance, and giving the war whoop; in which every ones voice was extended to its utmost capacity. At the close B ob-a-she-la; Bob-a-she-la with occasional broken English. Me shoot-me kill big Creek Injin, pointing to their scalp at the same time.

My uncle Daniel Huey (mother's brother) was in this war under Gen. Jackson, and returned to Fathers at the close very much debilitated: had been sick for some time. Mother took him in charge and by strictly dieting and nursing him he soon regained his health, and settled down as school teacher in Jefferson County on the Mississippi River, where he married and raised a family and amassed a considerable property which he finally sold and moved to Illinois or Indiana.

I think he always attributed the restoration of his health to Mother's feeding him on "Indian Sofkey", a dish which she learned to prepare from the Indians. The ingredients were, cracked corn, or hominy beaten in a mortar, boiled until done; with a certain portion of lye made from ashes. This was an excellent dish, a regulator of the stomach and bowels, and which if used now; would be far superior to thousands of nostrums that are selling in the country.

Father made a fair crop this year; as he generally did every year notwithstanding his frequent moves; and now prepared for another so that fall or winter he moved further down a few miles to the

- Gatlin place -

which was on the east side of the river, about five miles south of Bethel Church where he and mother held their membership and had done so from their first settlement in this county (Greene) and where they had worshiped all the time.

He remained at this place three years 1815-16 & 17 with the intention of buying it, whenever those lands wer offered for sale by the General Government. Which sale took place at St. Stephens on the Bigby River in either 1816 or 17. I think the latter. He went expecting to buy it, but when he got there found out the land would be run on him, and by one whom he had not the least cause to suspect, and one whom he always regarded as a true and fast friend and brother in the church. This of course had a bad effect upon his feelings, as well as his great surprise. He sought an interview with him, but could not get him to desist but they finally

22

agreed to divide the tract, and each one buy one half, which Father knew
was better for him than to have it put up and sold without some kind of
a compromise, knowing he was not able to compete with the other for the
whole of it. So accordingly it was sold in two lots, and each one got
the protion agreed upon in the compromise. Or it may have been all sold
in a body and one (his competitor I suppose) bought it and then divided it.

In the division however Father had to relinquish a good deal of the
land he wanted mostly; and considered it not at all in such a shape or
lying in such form as to make it desirable so at the end of 1817
or 1818 the same year that he bought it, sold it to Col. Morrison, at
a small profit I think at least did not lose by the transaction.

He made three crops here and generally good ones, and during this
time he had collected together, several head of stock cattle and hogs; and
in this way was increasing his means. But here a sad accident befell him;
he was badly bitten by a snake on the foot (a mockasin) from which he
came near loosing his life and but for the skill and attention of Dr.
Wheaton, it is presumable he would.

Here he was thrown among a kind, hospitable people such as Jacob
Neely and family, Durwell Rouse, Mrs. Roberts, Mrs. Morrison, Henry Roberts
and many others.

In the fall of 1818 I think it was, he with brother Andrew made a
visit to Tennessee to see his Father and relations; and on his return
brought with him a nephew, William N. Gracey, a son of one of his sisters,
who remained with us the next year, at our next home on the Pascagoula
River, and which refreshes my memory so that from this circumstance I know
that this visit to Tennessee was in 1818. The land also in the Spring and
his visit in the fall. During his stay at this place, there was held the
first camp meeting ever held in that country; which was held in 1817 at
Bethel and called afterwards McRae's Campground, it and the Church both
near his house. Father tented and a large congregation attended the
exercises all the time. This was the first of course I had ever seen, and
recollect now many amusing and strange things occured, but one of which
I will give. There were several preachers there officiating; among them
Thomas Griffin, as Presiding Elder, and Thomas Owens, and I think John J.
E. Byrd and others; Thomas Owens preached on Baptism, by the advice and
solicitation of the Presiding Elder (as I heard the older people say).

Editor's Note:

Page 22 - Daniel Huey, borther in law of William Ramsey, must have come
to the territory with the Ramsey family. His name appears on the
petition of the inhabitants to form Wayne County in 1809 just under
that of William Ramsey.
    Daniel Huey is listed as a private in Hinds Bn. of Cavalry, Mississ-
ippi Militia in _Mississippi Territory in the War of 1812_ by Mrs. Dunbar
Rowland.

page 22 - The Gatlin Place. It is difficult to determine which Gatlin
place is referred to at this point. Both Thomas and Edward Gatlin are
listed as owning land on the Chickasawhay River in Greene County, MS
on the Greene County Tax Rolls.

Page 22 and 23. Regarding the land William Ramsey wished to purchase
at the St. Stephens Land Office when it was offered for sale, the
person "running the land on him" was Isaac Roberts, Sr. See map on
page 26. This townshp plat of Greene County, MS shows both Isaac
Roberts and William Ramsey as owning this land and a purchase date of
1817. Portions of the township :'at of Greene County are missing.
The paper had disintegrated before the old map was found and taken to
the Mississippi Archives for microfilming. The portion copied on
page 25 is copied from this microfilm. Note other settlers nearby.

Page 23 - Col. Morrison referred to on this page could be any of the
following who are all on the Tax Rolls of Greene County, MS at this
time: Malcolm Morrison, Angus Morrison, Alexander Morrison and John D.
Morrison. Malcolm Morrison appears to be the older of the group and
the larger land owner.

Page 23 - Dr. Wheaton is Charles Wheaton. Charles Wheaton appears on the
1816 Territorial Census as over 21, with two sons, 3 daughters and wife,
and 8 slaves.

Page 23 - neighbors mentioned. Information taken from the 1816 Territorial
Census.
        Jacob Nealy - Males: 2 over 21, 1 under 21
                      Females: 1 over 21, 2 under 21   1 slave

        Burrell Rouse - Males: 1 over 21, 5 under 21
                      Females: 1 over 21, 2 under 21

        Millinda Roberts - Males: 3 under 21
                      Females: 1 over 21, 3 under 21

        Nancy Morrison - Males: 1 under 21
                      Females: 2 over 21, 1 under 21

        Henry Roberts is listed on the 1816 Tax Roll but not on the
        territorial census for 1816.

24

Editor's Note:

Page 23 - Visit to Tennessee by William Ramsey to see his father.

Passports of Southeastern Pioneers 1770 - 1823 by Dorothy Williams Potter
page 97   "Thomas A.Smith and William Ramsey have permission to pass
            thro the Cherokee Nation in their route to Georgia & Return —
            South West point   R. J. Meigs
            11th Nov.1802   A. War in Tennessee

"Some North Carolinians in the Revolutionary War who Moved to Mississippi"
North Carolina Genealogical Society Journal August 1985, compiled by
Betty S. Drake

RAMSAY, William (b. ca 1743, NC; d. GA or MS) Lived in Mecklenburg Co.,NC
during the Rev. War; service not verified because of several Wm. RAMSAY's
on NC rosters. Married Jemima _____. Descendants in Jackson County,MS
More concerning this William Ramsey can be found in Alice T. Welch's
Family Records Mississippi Revolutionary Soldiers and in Four Centuries
on the Pascagoula, Vols. 1 & 2 by Cyril E. Cain

Editor feels certain that William Ramsay (R.S.) did not die in Mississippi
and does not feel that he ever came to Mississippi and feels that death
occured in Tennessee

page 23 - Thomas Owens - see note page 20

County of *Greene* .. Township *1 North* Ra

His remarks I recollect clearly: On the application of the element
to the subject, said the preacher, "I baptize you _with_ water, what does
that mean but that the water is applied to the subject? If you were going
to whip one of your children how would you do it? Take the hickory and
apply it to the child! or would you lay the hickory on the ground, take
up the child by the heels and beat it over the switch. Or if you were
going to cut down that tree out there how would you do it? Apply the axe
to the tree, or the tree to the axe? Now the way we do, we whip the child
with the switch; cut the tree with the axe; and baptize the person _with_
water. But you reverse the thing altogether, you whip the switch with the
child, cut the axe with the tree, baptize the water with the subject. This
definition of this subject illustrated as it was made lasting impressions
on my young mind such as has never been effaced or driven from my memory.
I could easily understand by experience, the use of the word with when it
was used in application of the switch to the child, but thought if there
were such people on earth that reversed this order, and took the poor child
by the heels and beat him over the switch as the preacher said, how in
the world could they do such a thing, and if there were such I hoped I
might never get into their hands.

During one of the years we lived at this place either in 1815 or 1816
was the first time I had ever been introduced into a school, and which was
on this wise. My mother had taken great pains in learning me the alphabet
and some of the easy lessons in Noah Webster's spelling books and my brother
Andrew was going to school to an old Mr. Black, I was exceedingly anxious
to go with him. So to accomodate me, Mother accompanied me one afternoon
to the school house, which was on the opposite side of the river from
where we lived. When we came in sight of the institution, we heard the
scholars spelling and reading at the top of their voices, as loud as they
could with a word, a perfect Bable,confusion of tongues, which was the
custom in that day. Mother introduced me to the teacher as a new scholar
but only on trial, not knowing whether I could be satisfied with this new
order of things. The teacher, who by the by was a very good, clever old
man; assigned me my studies; with the command to the whole school "Get
your lessons" whereupon every one began as before at the top of their
voices and I with the rest, as loud as I could scream, for Mother had told
me I must do like the others, so at it I went. What I lacked in sense I

27

made up in noise, which was the case with others as well as me.

Mother left me that evening with brother Andrew, who boarded during the week at Mr. William Rivers. That evening's exercise was enough, I had my fill of the school, and wanted to go home; did not return to school any more. The next day Father came over and I went home "Graduated so far as Mr. Blacks school was concerned". Schools in those times, were generally what was called "three months or six months schools". So that when one teacher's term expired another was procured, provided the original one did not take the school for another term.

So on this instance Mr. Black's term expired, and a Mr. Perkins was engaged. Brother Andrew was continued as before. Mr. Black had been a very easy and endulgent teacher, too much so, to meet the prevailing popular opinions of that day, that an education must be beat into the pupils and that a teacher who did not use the rod freely, was no teacher at all. Black did not fill the bill, but Perkins did, with the masses at least. He was what was called a tight teacher, using the rod for every little delinquency, and one who would not be tolerated now. I accompanied brother Andrew on one occasion to this school, and was not there long, before the teacher gave a class of girls, nearly grown, some of them probably quite a severe whipping, with a chinquopin hickory, and during the day dressed out several of the boys. This did not suit me;I thought worse and worse; preferred Black with all the noise to Perkins and his hickorys, so I left, went home that evening which closed my school experience on the Chickasawha.

Recollections of Some of the Pioneer Preachers

I have already in another part of this sketch, alluded to this class who, under God, were the instruments of introducing and establishing on a permanent basis, the church of God and religion of Christ in this new country. But before leaving this neighborhood and community and tracing our steps to another new field and home, I wish to put on paper here some more distinct recollections of these holy men of God and their work; and particularly of one whose name has not been mentioned, viz "Richmond Nolly".

My first distinct recollection of these men, goes back to 1813 when Samuel Sellers as Presiding Elder and Richmond Nolly and John Shroak were sent into that country by the Western Conference. Nolley came from the South Carolina Conference. Previous to this year, the work there had been supplied by Missionaries from the South Carolina Conference. With such men (some of whom I have already alluded to) as Sturdivant, Burge, Kennon, Ford,

28

Editor's Notes:

Page 27 - "Old Mr. Black" was probably Hugh Black of Greene County, MS.

Page 28 - Mr. Perkins, the teacher, was probably John Perkins.

Both the Blacks and John Perkins are buried in Old Salem Cemetery in the woods in southern Greene County. John Perkins was born in Chesterfield District, S.C. on April 17, 1777 and died 10-2-1841 in Greene County, MS There is no marked grave for Hugh Black, however many members of the Black family are buried there. There are 15 to 20 unmarked graves in this cemetery. The cemetery is located near the site of Salem Church. At one time a large school was located here; later than the time period Ramsey is referring to in his narrative.

Page 28 - For biographical sketches of Presiding Elders and preachers, see History of Methodism in Alabama by Lazenby and History of Methodism in Mississippi by John G. Jones.

Houston, Quinn.

Samuel Sellers was a large man, of more than medium height, florid complexion, red or rather auburn hair, rather a rough countenance and had the appearance of one able to do the work assigned to him; a good preacher and acceptable with the people. (For this estimate of his virtues I am indebted to older ones, whose opinions I had as I grew up).

Richmond Nolley, was a small, spare made, pale face man, black eyes and hair, rather weakly in appearance and strength. I met a few ywars ago, at the conference at Talladega, a facsimile to the best of my recollection of Richmond Nolley's countenance and physiognomy; in the person of Bishop Marvin; I mean his face. The Bishop was a larger man, but the shape and form of his nose and face, color of hair & eyes &c struck me forcibly, as soon as I saw him, of being very much like Nolley.

Richmond Nolley was one, among many, of the most devoted consecrated and holy men of God, I presume I ever saw. Such were his habits of abstenance and fasting that being of a weakly constitution that his brethern had fears that he was doing wrong; and so advised him, and insisted on his taking more nourishment; that he was pursuing a course, although conscientiously, would terminate in disease and probably death; and thereby cut off his usefulness to the church and the cause in which he was engaged. His reply would generally be "That is between me and my God." He was a man of prayer of reading and study; never unemployed; never triflingly employed. Made the woods and groves wherever he went, and where there was no private room that he could command, his study, reading the Bible upon his knees. Frequently have I seen him in his private studies and devotions, when at my father's whose place was one of his stopping places. And often his hand on my head and gave me such advice and counsel as was adapted to my age. I loved Uncle Nolley and still cherish the remembrance of his many Christian virtues, with warm and affectionate recollections. This good man's career was short, but no doubt triumphant. Found by the road side upon his knees frozen to death, on the west side of the Mississippi River.

John Shrock was a low, well set, healthy looking man, black eyes and hair, apparently a young man; one who had the appearance of being adapted to pioneer and missionary work. From my recollections of him, I would suppose him to be of German extract; a good faithful preacher and acceptable with the people.

30

Some time that year 1813, a quarterly meeting was held at Bethel
Church where the Presiding Elder (Sellers) and the two preachers (assistant
preachers they were called then) Nolley and Schrock were in attendance.
A part of the exercises I distinctly recollect. Love feast was to be held
Sunday morning, before preaching. More rigid care was exacted then than
now, in admitting persons to this prudential means of grace. Tickets were
issued to all who wished to partake, and against whom no objections were
interposed. A sentinel was placed at the door, to guard against unaccept-
able persons, and receive tickets. Old Father McRae was the appointed
sentinel that morning. I was standing hard by, looking and noticing the
proceedings when a certain lady (sister I suppose) approached with a very
nice looking feather in her bonnet. Father McRae very mildly remarked to
her "Sister you can't come in here with that feather in your bonnet."
The good sister very deliberately took off her bonnet, pulled the feather
out, put it up in a crack of the house (being a log house) and went in,
and no doubt enjoyed the occasion much more than she would have done
otherwise.

I have often thought of this love feast, and the rules by which they
were then governed, in contrast with such occasions now. Well may we
exclaim "Ichabod" the glory of the Methodist church has departed, in this
as well as in other things. Love feasts, Class meetings, and communion
service were in those days and for a long time afterwards seasons of refresh-
ing, of joy, of spiritual strength to the church and often producing convictions among the people of the world. People did not have to be begged
and teased to attend upon these services, and then laboured with to arise
and speak for the Master, and stand as a witness for the truth, but regarded it a privilege, yea, a great privilege to testify to the truth of our
holy christianity. O Lord help the church to enquire for the old paths
and walk therein.

The next presiding elder that came among us as successor to Samuel
Sellers in 1817 was Thomas Griffin and with him, I think, as assistants
were J. I. E. Byrd and Thomas Owens to all of whom allusion has already
been made.

Thos. Griffin was a long, lank, raw boned man; heavy eye browed; a
keen eye, daring countenance, courageous, independant in thought and deed.
His motto was be sure I am right and the right pursue. He was an uncom-
promising opponent to all classes of vice, but especially to gambling and

31

the use of intoxicating liquors. His public expositions of the vices rendered him unpopular with their adherents, yet but little did he care; the truth he would proclaim in the face of any opposition, from the world, the flesh, and the devil. J. I. E. Byrd was a little over ordinary size, round, compact form, keen eye, roman nose, affable manners, an affectionate temperment, plain, practical, forcible, and useful preacher. Here he became associated in marriage with Miss Margaret McRae, daughter of Father John McRae. The precise year of his marriage I do not now remember for he was on that circuit I think more than once, if not in succession at intervals until 1823. He finally lost his eyesight, became blind and lived and preached to a good old age, and died a few years ago in Mississippi.

Thomas Owens was a small, lean, long faced, good forehead, keen eyed, little preacher, a nervous temperment, a man of great fortitude, fearless, did not court the applause or smiles of a sinful world, battled against error in all its forms and phases, done much good, preached pointedly and forcibly to the hear, and not so much to the head. And almost invariably supplemented his sermons by inviting penitents forward for prayer; and to use one of his own phrases (I believe it was) generally wound up with a "ground scuffle". He was quite an eccentric man, in actions and expressions. Many amusing scenes have been told of his passing through; and many anecdotes as taking place with him. He lived to a good ripe old age, and died a few years ago in Mississippi.

These with many others of their contemporaries and successors I could trace were it necessary, and had I the minutes of the conference from 1813 to 1829, and speak of them from personal knowledge and recollection, but this would crowd my sketch to too great a size, beside add but little probably, to its merit or usefulness. Hence I will close this part, by one general commendation and tribute to these worthy men of God "who being dead yet speaketh" and "whose works follow them".

No person of common reasoning facilities could attribute to these men a pure selfish and personal motive; such as would lead them to submit to the sacrifices and hardships to which they were now subjected. Neither could ease, affluence, wealth or fame have controlled them. To leave kindred, home and friends in a distant state, to go out from the sacred and endearing ties which naturally bound them to the homes, society and habits of the old settled communities; and with no other earthly reward in view

32

than the persecutions, trials, afflictions and poverty incident to such
a life, and the prospect of want staring in the face, and probably a watery
grave, and at best a burial in some lone sequestered spot inhabited by
savages and beast of prey, and not money enough accumulated by the enterprise to afford them decent clothes, and a decent Christian burial,
provided they should fall among a civilized class. Could it have been
ease, contentment, honor, fame, riches and self aggrandizement; pleasure
and worldly happiness that moved and became the controlling principle
to their actions? Common sense and common reason says nay! We must look
for motives higher and deeper than those which we have examined and which
are merely sublemary. It was the Love of Christ and his cause, an ardent
desire for the salvation of man; and an abiding sense of the obligations
imposed upon them to preach the Gospel, as far as in their power, to every
creature. Going forth then under these convictions of duty, and trusting
the blessed Saviour, who had promised to be with them to end of the world;
they went forth not knowing what might befall them; and planted the standard
of the cross; sowed the seed; laid the foundation, of a spiritual superstructure which has since risen to its present commanding attitude, where
we see church houses; campgrounds; Family altars raising their enviable
walls and sending forth their strains of prayer and praise in almost
every hamlet, town and neighborhood, where these pioneers first proclaimed
the Truth.

- Our Next Home -

was in Jackson County, on the west side of the Pascagoula River at the
Bates place and owned by a Col. Bates, who had left it and moved to the
Bigby River. This place was about two miles south of Hudson's Ferry (now
Fairley's) and immediately in the neighborhood of Jacob Holland, Sr.,
Charles Holland, Peter Fairly, Esq., Thomas Bilbo, Isaac Ryan, Aaron Parker,
Neil Little, Mrs. Little, John Deas, the Cochran's, Cowart's and others.
A fine, hospitable, honest, industrious, and in the main, pious community.

Here we lived until the Winter of 1820, cultivating fine river bottom
lands, which was very productive and on which Father made good crops. But
being subject to inundation, very uncertain as to the harvest.

In 1819 Father's crop of corn was very fine; but a freshet in the latter
part of August, completely covered the field except a few high ridges; the
corn being nearly dry, but in a state to sour and rot, but little of it was
saved in a condition that could be used. And what was saved was mostly

33

Editor's Notes:

Page 33 — "Bates Place and Col. Bates. No evidence is found of Bates owning land in this area in the land records. However, this was probably Thomas Bates who had previously lived in Washington County, M.T. (AL) and who probably returned to that area after a brief stay on the Pascagoula River.

The property, according to Ramsey, was located about two miles south of Hudson's Ferry. This would put it in Section 27, Township 2 South, Range 8W in present day George County, MS. Hudson's land was located in Section 22, Township 2S, Range 8W. This would be about a mile south of Benndale, MS.

Charles and Jacob Holland — Charles Holland's land was located in Section 36, Township 2 South, Range 8W. No sectional description could be found for Jacob Holland, but he is listed as a land owner.

Peter Fairley, Neil Little, Mrs. Little, do not appear on the list of actual settlers in the district prior to the 3rd of March 1819. This list was actually promulgated in 1820.

Thomas Bilbo is shown as living in Section 43, township 2N, Range 8W and in Section 41, township 2N, Range 8W. Section 41 is on the west side of the Pascagoula and section 43 on the east side. Land in this area is not divided in the traditional 36 section township because of the irregular Spanish and English land grants in the area before it became a part of the United States.

An entry on 13 July 1804 in the earliest deed book of Washington County, M.T. shows that Thomas Bilbo and Ann Lawrence were married by John Callier, J.P.

Isaac Riand (Ryan) is shown as owning land in Section 12, Township 3S, Range 8 in 1812. For a very informative and well documented article on Isaac Ryan see "A Ryan Heritage" by Brother Jerome Lepre, S.C., Journal of the Jackson County Genealogical Society, Vol. 1, No. 1, page 4.

Aaron Parker's land was located in section 40, townshp 2, range 8W.

The Cochran's were, no doubt, the family of William and Margaret Cochran who had come to the territory from Barnwell District, S.C. William Cochran had land in Section 3, Township 1 south, Range 8 West and his son Burwell or Burrell had land in section 3, Township 1 south, Range 8 West.

The Cowart's were Ezekiel Cowart and his extensive family. Ezekiel Cowart had land in Section 25, Township 1, Range 8W. He had come from Barnwell District, S.C. where he had married Margaret Cochran, daughter of William and Margaret Cochran above.

John Deas — John Deas had land in Section 3, Township 2 South, Range 8 West on the west side of the Pascagoula River. An entry on 12 July 1805 in the first Deed Book of Washington County, M.T.(AL) shows that a pre-nuptial agreement was recorded prior to the marriage of John Deas and Bridget Burk, a widow (widow of William Burk).

done by getting skiffs & ferry boats; and wading, diving, and swimming and
thereby collecting or pulling it and carrying it to the high lands, where
it was exposed to the sun to be dried, but all to little purpose, mostly
rotted. The result of this mode of harvesting a crop, connected with the
germs of fever produced by this late overflow of the large swamps that lay
near us, produced a bad state of health in the family; chills and fever;
shaking agues, took hold of several members of the family, and among them
was Uncle John Huey who lived with us that year, and who had a long and
severe attack; besides other members of the family.

The year before this 1818, Cousin W. N. Gracey, to whom allusion has
already been made, lived with us and during that year he embraced religion
under the ministry of Rev. J. I. E. Byrd who was on the circuit that year.
At the close of the year Cousin Gracey left and went back to Tennessee,
where he attached himself to the Cumberland Presbyterian Church and became
a minister in that denomination.

Among the many kind and accomodating neighbors in that community,
I hope I shall not be charged with "drawing any invidious distinctions, by
noticing that of John Deas, an Irishman, and staunch and unflinching Roman
Catholic. He owned and lived at the place where Judge John Fairley subsequently lived and died.

He had married a methodist wife, a widow Burke, who had two sons,
Charles and James Burke, at their marriage. Two other sons Oliver and
Edward were the offspring of their marriage. These four boys became
school mates of mine during the two years we lived there.

Mr. Deas was as kind, hospitable and charitable a man as could be
desired in any community. A man of great reading and information, particularly in regard to the tenets of the Roman Catholic Church; loved argument
and never better delighted than when he could get the company of some
Protestant with whom he could controvert their peculiar theories. He
generally attended service at the Methodist Church and invariably invited
the preachers home with him. And woe be unto the young man, whose reading,
studies and general information, disqualified him to meet the arguments
of this Giant of Catholicism. But Deas did not like, he said, to argue
with boys. He wanted old men, men of experience, of learning, men who knew
something, and would remark "these young men don't know anything." And
such were his love for argument on this theme, that some of the yound preachers appeared to be afraid of him and refuse going to his house.

It was told of him, that on one occasion, when Rev. Samuel Walker was on the circuit, Deas had invited him home with him several times and he had refused to go, that finally anticipating the cause, said he to the preacher, "I do believe you are afraid of me, come along, I'm not going to hurt you, I know you are young, don't know much, you are not the sort of man I want. The sort I am after for an argument .. send along old Tom Griffin; he's the kind I want to get ahold of." But withal his Catholic proclivities, he was honest in his convictions, honest in his intercourse with men, benevolent and charitable, and worthy citizen and neighbor. He sold his place there to Judge John Fairley of North Carolina and removed to Perry County on Leaf River, where I last saw him, and shared in his hospitality in 1832. I could say much on commendation of the many kind people of this community, but it would crowd my notes to too great a length to be interesting to any one.

In 1818 a school was organized, not far from us, on the main public River road; leading up and down the river. About one half mile from Peter Fairley's mill and about the same distance from the Methodist Church and graveyard both of which lay west of the school house. A very central location commanding the patronage of miles around, including the neighborhoods on the river from Thomas Bilbos south to John Deas north. Enrolling I suppose twenty five or thirty scholars, or more. Some coming three to three & a half miles. In this school Father entered four scholars, Bro. Andrew, Sister Ann, bro. William, and myself.

      - An Inside Look into this School and So On

This was taught by Mr. Neill Little, a brother in law of Peter Fairley, Esq. and but recently from North Carolina, a Scotchman. Here were thrown together, as pupils, all sizes and ages, from little boys and girls to grown young men and women; and of course as different in temperaments and dispositions as in their ages and sizes; and many of whom had probably never been in school before. Hence the oversight and control of these different elements and to so adapt the management and discipline so as to accomplish the desired and contemplated end, was to the teacher no doubt, a subject of deep concern. But believing himself master of the situation, and sufficiently competent for the task, he arranged and marshalled his classes, promulgated his rules and went to work. The next thing in order was to introduce a large chinquapin hickory in the school room; much to the alarm

Editor's Note:

page 36 - Judge John Fairley - An excellent article on this family may be found in the Journal of the Jackson County Genealogical Society, Vol. II, no. 2, "Echoes from the Past" by Nap Cassibry. This article gives an old court case in 1859 which was decided by the Supreme Court. It spans an area from the late 1700s to 1859 and gives much genealogy of the Fairley family.

Page 36 - School taught by Mr. Neill Little. This paragraph gives the location of a Methodist Church and cemetery. Using the fact that Judge John Fairley purchased the land of John Deas which was located in Section 3, Township 2 South, Range 8 West, we can assume that Fairley's mill was located on Mill Creek which runs through this section thereby giving the Creek its name. The Methodist church and cemetery is probably the beginning of Antioch Methodist Church which is now located in Section 28, Township 2 south, Range 8 west. The present location of Antioch Methodist Church dates back to 1825. It is tradition that the church began earlier than 1825 and that it was probably located north or west of the present location. Taking tradition, Ramsey's comments and description, it is logical to believe that Antioch Methodist Church began in 1818 and that its location was probably 3 to 3½ miles north of its present day location, thereby making it the oldest church in George County.

and fright of the little ones, if not to some of the larger ones also.
Very soon afterwards, he discovered to the school he knew how to handle
this hickory, which gave to some such a scare that they never learned any
thing during the whole school. The small children, some of them at least,
had better been at home. For his unheard of rules and his severity kept
the school in a perfect state of dread and excitement, particularly the
smaller ones.

Some of his rules, were simply ridiculous, unheard of, not calculated
in their execution to accomplish any good whatever, but to consume time
which should have been employed in study by the scholars; and which often
produced in the minds of some a disposition of insubordination and sometimes levity and disobedience rendering it necessary, as he thought, to
use the rod and generally severly.

One of those rules was, on many occasions for delinquency in duty,
or study or a correct and prompt recitation of the lesson, a jury was
empanelled and sent out to try the case of the culprit; a regular foreman
appointed, and on whose decision or verdict, he would act. Inflicting
such punishment as the jury had adjured; which was, of course, not every
time decided upon the merits of the case; but frequently from personal
spleen which some of the jurors bore towards the accused.

Another rule was, to allow them to give security for good behavior,
or better recitations in the future. This rule was generally, and almost
invariably brought to bear upon the smaller boys and girls. And often have
I seen them going round crying and begging the larger ones to stand for
them.

Fortunately for me, I never was put to the painful necessity or of
being tried by a jury. I was as afraid of him as I would have been of a
bear. Constantly in dread. Kept my mind and eyes constantly on my book
and was never subjected to any of his silly modes of punishment, but once,
and that was for missing to spell correctly a word, and which was
"Hatteras" I never shall forget it. I left out one t and spelt it Hateras,
and but one trial allowed. He had another unheard of rule which he brought
me under that day. Which was for the offender to hold out his hand, at
arms length, and make one of the little boys or girls take his hickory,
and cut them in the hand; and which generally resulted in a laugh at the
little fellows grinning, smiling, and grunting at the awkwardness and em-
barrasment of their situation, in correction larger ones. On the occasion,

38

he appointed little Roderick Mathison to execute the law on me and my class
of two others, both of whom had failed on other words.

The poor frightened, scared little fellow made so many wry faces,
grunted, and tried so many ways to get out of it that it caused the teacher
to laugh heartily and of course the whole school. I scarcely felt the
lick; the little fellow was very lenient. Here was fifteen or twenty
minutes lost time in this nonsensical farce.

Another mode of punishment was to threaten and even attempt to hang
some of the little ones; particularly little Roderick Matheson (already
referred to) and Edward Dean, two of the smallest and youngest boys in
school.

I saw him upon one occasion, take off his suspenders tie them around
little Matheson's neck and raise him from the floor, so that the little
fellow, was nearly strangled before he let him down. At another time he
tied his suspenders around little Edward Dean neck and started off to the
spring when he told him there was a large limb on a white oak, which was
his gallows and on which he intended to hang him. But the little fellow,
in his efforts and struggles to get loose from him finally succeeded and
ran to the house. Here his half brother Charles Burke a grown young man
interposed and said to him, "this thing had to be stopped, he had carried
it as far as he intended it should be". The teacher submitted and well
for him he did, for if he had not, the probabilities are that mischief
would have been done. These two little boys never learned anything during
the six months Little taught that school.

It has always been to me a matter of astonishment how our parents
submitted to this man's mode of government in that school. My very nature
now while giving this partial description of it, recoils within me. Such
a man in a schoolroom now, to attempt such a course, would be hissed out
of the community, if nothing worse; would not, nor could not be tolerated.
Nor was his course endorsed by the people there any longer than the term
for which he engaged. He was informed that he was not wanted there any
longer and the patrons engaged Alexander Fairly, who took charge and
proved to be an acceptable teacher to parents and children. A marked improvement in the advances of his scholars was seen developed, especially
with those smaller ones who through fear and fright had made a perfect
failure before, now advanced and learned well under the mild, persuasive,
and reasonable discipline of Mr. Fairley.

I mention these schools to show the disadvantages arising from un-
reasonable discipline, and a want of proper care and study of the different
dispositions and temperaments of children upon the part of teachers, so
as to adapt their discipline and management to the different classes of
mind committed to their care. And also to show the utility and benefits
growing out of a proper understanding and appreciation of the fact that
different minds require different treatment in intellectual culture,
as well as in other matters. And which was exemplified in these two schools.
Before I dismiss this school, I ask permission to mention one other incident
which occured with Mr. Little's jury trials, and which slipped my memory
at the time I referred to this part of his administration. - - It happened
that on one occasion a class consisting of Jesse Holder who boarded at
Fathers and some few others, among whom was Jane Bilbo, missed their
lessons, could not recite it. A jury was empanelled with Edward Deas
foreman: the court delivered the charge: they retired: very soon returned
when the court addressed them; "That they all stand in the center of the
floor until the whole school says their lessons round" which was executed,
much to the chagrin of that class. On the next day, poor little Ed Deas
became the subject of jury investigation. Jesse Holder and his class were
selected jurors. Jesse, Foreman: after the usual charge of the court, they
retired and in a few minutes returned with smiles on their faces, apparently
exulting in the chance for retaliation. The court "Well Mr. Foreman what
is your verdict?" "Hang him, Sir", says Holder, and retired to their seats,
saying silently to themselves, no doubt, "now, Sir, that is what you get
by keeping us standing up in the floor an hour when you could have cleared
us."

I dismiss this school narrative by adding that this was an isolated
case. No other teacher who taught me afterwards, or I ever heard of in
my long experience and observation, ever adopted such measures or in the
least attempted to imitate the example here introduced in the first organization of schools in that newly settled country.

- Our Last and Final Move, and Reasons For It -

Father had now become afflicted, which finally terminated in a disease
that completely rendered him helpless, and which had been coming on him
for some time, the Palsey, I suppose it was. And from which he never
recovered, and became a perfect helpless invalid for many years before his

Editor's Notes:

page 39 - Roderick Matheson is probably the son of James Matherson who is
listed in the 1820 census of Jackson County, MS as having 3 sons under
10 and 2 age 10 to 16. The correct spelling of the surname is uncertain.

Page 39 - Edward Deas son of John Deas and his wife Bridget Burke.
Charles Burke - half brother of Edward Deas and son of Bridget Burke by
her first marriage to William Burke. She was a widow with 2 sons when
she married John Deas in Washington County, M.T.

page 39 - Alexander Fairley was related to Peter Fairley, brother in
law of Neal Little, the first teacher at this school. Peter Fairley
married Margaret Little and later lived in Perry County, MS.
Alexander Fairley lived in Perry County, MS later also. The 1850 census
of Perry County, MS lists him as born in NC ca 1797. He married Margaret
Thompson who was also from NC.

Page 40 - Jesse Holder son of Willis Holder of Jackson County, MS. Willis
Holder had 2 sons under 10 in 1820 and one son 10 to 16. Willis Holder
moved to Jasper County and died there.

Page 41 - Jane Bilbo daughter of Thomas Bilbo.

death; so much so that he could neither walk, dress or feed himself.
Having about this time while living at this river place bought a piece
of land on White Sand Creek, in Lawrence County, on Pearl River which he
intended settling, but anticipating the state of his future health and
the probabilities of his not being able to open up a farm on this newly
acquired tract of land, sold it for stock — cattle and sheep. These in
connection with what he already had gave him as he thought (and correctly
to) a pretty good start of stock and consequently decided to move to the
range and give up trying to make a living by cultivating river lands. So
in the fall of that year, either 1818 or 1819 he gathered up his cattle,
hogs and sheep and drove them to the range on the south side of Red Creek
in the neighborhood of Willis Holders, a distance of about twenty miles.
Selected him a place in the woods; a beautiful bluff on the said Red Creek
about four miles west of Mr. Holders. Went to work, built his house, which
consisted of two log houses, with a passage between them. A kitchen was
provided also and subsequently other buildings were added, after our move
there and which made it a comfortable home such as was common in that
country at that day. This place was surrounded with a beautiful picturesque
ridge of white sand hills, covered over with saw palmetto, prickly pears,
and black jack timber, belting the large level cove of pine lands within
its limits forming an area of a half mile square, immediately on this bluff
running back from the creek to the sand hill and furnishing near by in one
hundred yards an excellent spring of as fine water as run out of the
earth. If my recollection be correct we landed there at this new place on
the 23rd of February 1820 or may have been one year earlier 1819, but my
convictions are it was the former date. In moving thither two large Creeks
(as they were called) besides some smaller ones intervene. Black Creek,
Red Creek, and Bluff Creek were the most formidable. And on these no
ferries had as yet been established. Canoes were the only modes of convey-
ing persons, goods and chattels and vehicles across, while stock had to
be swam across.

These difficulties and obstructions however, were finally overcome
and we landed safely at home in the pine woods. But O the prospect! Here
to be put down, where there was no road leading in any direction except
a blind path recently made, leading to Mr. Holder's and the crossing place
on Red Creek, and which had been somewhat beaten down and opened by our
moving over it. No neighbors except Mr. Holder four miles distant; surrounded by wild beasts and game of different kinds such as bear, panther,

wild cats, wolves, foxes & c, whose depredations on sheep, lambs, hogs
and cattle were not unfrequent. No mills nearer than where we moved from,
all provisions needed have to be brought from there on horse back made the
appearance of things and prospect of living a gloomy and discouraging one.
Coupled with this, was the corps of effective labourers to improve this
place and do the manual labour and drudgery. This consisted of Anunt
Dinah, Bro. Andrew and myself both of us small, not grown, and unable to
do but little. Bro. A being about 14 and I a little diminutive, sickley,
asthmatic creature, could do nothing that required strength, muscle and
nerve. Father's condition such as rendered him almost entirely inefficient.
Hence the future presented anything but a bright side, particularly so to
Mother, but she had been accustomed to "hard times" and close places; and
consequently did not complain, but took courage trusting as formerly in
God, who had promised that "her bread should be given her and her water
should be sure."

But while these clouds of discouragements loomed up before us, there
were some mitigating circumstances, calculated to inspire hope, and render
the situation a little more cheerful. Our stock of cattle that roamed
around us looked fine and fat; the grass, thisck, long and tender, the
ravins or branches, creek bottoms, covered with a thick cane or reed
brake; no frost had fallen to kill of the luxuriant grass which then
covered and carpeted the large plateaus of pine forest that spread out for
miles, over which the fire had been caused to run and consume the old,
to make place for the new crop. This looked cheering and inviting. So
that very soon our table abounded with those agreeable and healthy
luxuries "milk, butter and cheese."

As to meats, no scarcity. Fat beef, pork, venison, turkey and fish
whenever needed. And to those who desired it bear, panther, wild cats,
opossum and coon meats could be and were often procured in abundance.

The hog range here was equal to the necessities of the people, requiring no corn to prepare them for pork.

For several years, large fine fat porkers could be killed from the
woods. One great difficulty in rearing this species of stock was the
prevalence of so many destructive wild beasts that inhabited the large,
dense swamps of the country. But these were finally broken up to a large
extent by the settling up of the country and generally by a class of men
that took delight and enjoyed the sport of hunting these down with dogs
and guns.

And here, I must not neglect to say a word in favor of two distinguished dogs that father had procured and took with him to this place. Rover and Driver, both curs and brothers. But for their vigilant watch, indomitable courage, and love of hunting, their sagacity, sense and persevering disposition to hunt down, capture and kill the many wild animals they met with from a possum to a bear, I do not know how we could have lived there and raised any stock at all of hog, sheep, calves or chickens.

I have often known them to go off by themselves, tree some animal, at such a distance, where we could not hear their barks and lie by it until they became starved for something to eat before they would leave and come home. Whenever in hearing, we invariably went to their relief and never were we disappointed in finding either a panther, wild cat or a smaller animal such as fox or coon; not often a bear for they scarcely every took a tree. It happened upon two occasions the first year we lived here that a panther came at one time at night in fifty yards of the gate and jumped on a hog in its bed; the dogs were there in an instant at the squeal of the hog, which was rescued, and the dogs pursuing the animal soon had him on a tree. There they remained until morning when father, who was then able to walk, brother Andrew and myself went to their relief and after two or three jumps from the trees where the dogs had pushed him to, bro. Andrew slipped up on him and dispatched him. The other case was about 10 o'clock in the morning a hog squealed near the house; the dogs were there immediately run him up a tree. A young man Sandy Nicholson, who was making shoes for us, and I ran and he soon brought down a fine, large panther, but in the scuffle with the dogs which had laid hold of him, he had like to have killed poor Driver, by giving his throat a severe cut with his claws laying the wind pipe bare in three places, with three of his long sharp claws. Two such dogs I never saw before not have I since. They lived to a good old age, had been bitten, mangled, nearly killed by bear and panthers several times, and I believe were finally killed by a bear, one of them at least.

It may be considered foolishness in me to put this in my narrative, but I do it as a tribute of respect to the memory of old Rover and Driver who were the house guard and life guard of the family and the protector of those domestic animals that were then the source of our support.

      - Our Church Privileges -

From these we were now cut off, for a time. No church house, no
church organization, no preaching, nearer than at the church on the river
from which we had removed, which Father and Mother would occasionally
attend. But as a temporary supply of this want, Father, who had been acting for a long time in the capacity of Class Leader, and which office he
held as long as he was able to attend to its duties, appointed prayer
meetings at Mr. Holders, some of which he conducted at night. The congregation of grown persons consisted of Mr. & Mrs. Holder, himself and Mother.
Mr. Holder was not at that time a professor of religion, his wife was.
But very soon after the establishment of these prayer meetings, he became interested and seriously convicted, and at one of these prayer meetings at night, and in his own house he was converted and rejoiced in the
consciousness of sins forgiven and his acceptance with God. He attached
himself to the church soon after, where Father and Mother and Mrs. Holder
held their membership on the river and became a consistent, faithful working Christian in the cause of Christ; and finally at the organization of
a Society, or Church in our neighborhood succeeded Father as class leader.
One incident in his conversion is worthy of being preserved. Before it
he could not sing; was never known as he said himself to sing or carry a
tune; but on his sudden change of heart, mind and feelings, the power of
song was given him and he became a good singer, and in which service he
took great delight. In the fall of 1836, he moved to Jasper County where
he died, in faith, leaving behind him the order of a pure Christian life
and example.

Soon after this, through his and Father's influence, a preaching
place was procured, six or eight miles from us at the private house of
Solomon Dearmon's which was situated between Red and Black Creeks on or
near Bluff Creek, and not far from the road leading to the river settlement;
and the services of the preacher on that circuit, were procured, to attend
once in every four weeks on work days. This was quite a relief and here
for two years we attended preaching and I believe the nucleus of a society
formed, consisting of Father,Mother, Mr and Mrs. Holder, Mr. and Mrs.
Dearmon and probably some of their children.

The first preacher that attended and preached there was Wiley Ledbetter
in 1821; then a distinguished preacher of the Mississippi Confernece, a
man of great force and power but who, for some cause, I know not what,

finally fell, and was expelled from the conference. The last time I
saw him was at his home in Perry County; and at a wedding in his neighborhood, where I was called on to marry a Mr. Reed to a Miss Myers in 1836.
He had entirely given up religion and was trying to embrace infidelity.
I remonstrated with him; referred him to what he once was; the good that
he had tried to accomplish, and in which no doubt he had succeeded; referred to his preaching to me when a little boy, but all to no effect;
a few years afterward I heard he had died. O how appropriate the exhortation of the Apostle "He that thinketh he standeth take heed lest he fall".

The next one, who preached there was Edmund Pearson* in 1822, compar-
atively a young man, but very acceptable; a man as well as I now can
recollect of considerable promise to the church and who afterwards filled
many important appointments in that and the Alabama Conference, after it
was set off from the Mississippi Conference.

These preachers, however, did not attend here regularly, their visits,
if my memory is correct, were only occasional. This was an outside
appointment, not included in the regular circuit. And how long, or how
many years elapsed while our neighborhood and community had to submit to
these privations before we were regularly taken into the circuit of the
Leaf River and favored with the regular services of the preachers appointed
thereon. I do not distinctly recollect, but think it was not very long
before Bro. Holder and Father built a comfortable school house on the half
way ground between them, which served the double purpose of a church house,
and which has been no uncommon thing in the Methodist church from its first
organization and introduction into this country to be compelled to substi-
tute school houses for churches and in many of which souls have been converted and made happy under the preaching of the word, and from the walls
of which, ministers of the Gospel have been sent out who have blessed the
world and become shining lights in the church of God.

It is impossible for me now, at this advanced period, to give in
regular order, the details as to time, the years & c of the many incidents
I am endeavoring to record. Hence I can only mention the facts and incidents of many without a correct knowledge of recollection of the time of
their occurence.

During the period, to which I have referred, as being deprived of
the regular stated means of grace, dispensed by the Ministers of the

*Note: Thos. Owens & Edmund Pearson was on the Chickasawha Circuit in 1822.

Gospel; prayer meetings and class meetings were kept up; and due regard
of the sanctity of the Holy Sabbath and attendance upon family prayers
constantly enjoined. All of which tended to impress our young minds with
religious truth, and inspire a reverence for God and his word, as well
as confidence, in the piety of those, from whom these parental lessons
emanated.

Soon after the erection of the School House referred to, we were
visited by the itinerant preachers, and taken into the circuit.. The
first one that served that appointment was old brother Edward Harper in
1824. An elderly man, who had been preaching a number of years, a man
full of faith and the Holy Ghost; a useful acceptable preacher. He had
in company with him, one or two rounds on his circuit, a local preacher,
by the name of Jacob Colley, a bachelor, had no family and spent the
most of his time riding round with the preachers; a man who had read a
good deal, but a cold, phlegmatic speaker, never accomplished much good.
It was told that on one occasion Uncle Ned Harper in conversation with
Colley, said to him "Jake, if you don't get to heaven, you ought to go
to Hell! For a man to have as easy a time in this life as you,no family
care, no troubles, and nothing to harass the mind and ride about and get
your living, and nothing to do but serve God; if you don't do it and get
to Heaven, you ought to be damned". Jake laughed and quietly remarked
"I hope I shall get to Heaven."

I never heard but one objection, to Uncle Ned Harper and that was by
those who loved a free Gospel, and whose feelings against the preacher
were generally excited, if he said anything about money, about his quarter-
age. Old Uncle Ned would ask them for it, this some did not like. Let
it be borne in mind that the law of the church, allowed only to a man $100.00
and the same to his wife, if he had one, and a small allowance to each
child under such an age; and in those times there were generally no efficient
board of Stewards, and consequently the preacher, if he got anything had
to be his own Steward; and as such Uncle Ned had to act for himself, and
I presume he knew how, and was not afraid to let his wants be known.

The next one on that Circuit was Miles Harper, in 1825, no relation
to Uncle Ned, however. Neither was there any similarity in the two men.
Miles was an excellent preacher to a large congregation; loved big folks,
and big things;passionately fond of good eating. A little too high and

Note: The Leaf River circuit was formed in 1823. Zachariah Williams, P.C.
in 1823; 1824 Edward Hawkins.

47

Editor's Notes:

Page 44 - Sandy Nicholson - Alexander Nicholson of Perry County, MS.
The year is probably 1823 for it appears Alexander Nicholson reached
his majority this year. Son of Peter Nicholson of Perry County who
reportedly drowned in the Pearl River.

Page 45 - Solomon Dearmon - 1820 census of Jackson County shows the
following:
      Solomon Dearman - Males: 1 under 10, 1(10-16), 1(16-26), 1(26-45)
                        Females: 2 under 10, 2(16-26), 1(26-45)
The Dearmon family was from Craven and Anson Counties, NC by way of
Darlington District, SC to Alabama and Mississippi very early.

Page 45 - Mr. & Mrs. Holder - Willis Holder and wife.

Page 45 - Wiley Ledbetter is listed in the 1820 census of Lawrence
County, MS; 1830 census of Hinds County, MS; and by 1840 is living in
Perry County, MS. In 1840 Census he is listed as age 70 to 80 and his
wife is age 60 - 70. No children are listed in household.   .

Page 46 - Marriage of Mr. Reed to Miss Myers in 1836 in Perry County, MS
This is John B. Reed (spelled Read in census) born ca 1816 in England
married Ann Myers born in Georgia ca 1816. Their children were Daniel,
born 1838; Rachel, born 1839; Eliza, born 1841, married in 1868 Caleb
McDonald; Sarah, born 1845; and Margaret born 1851, married 1876 Thomas
Franklin Rawls.

Church & School House built by Willis Holder and William Ramsey may have
been the church referred to as being at Wolf Pitt. It is known that
there was a church earlier than Red Hill Methodist Church which was
begun in 1837. The earlier church was said to be at Wolf Pitt.

See History of Methodism in Mississippi and History of Methodism in
Alabama for biographical sketches of ministers.

48

elevated, in his thoughts and manners, for poor folks in the piney woods.
When he first came round, he didn't appear to care much, whether the people
went to heaven or hell. Before the year was out, however, he became
quite sociable and pliant. He lost his horse that year accidently or
rather by carelessly tieing it in old Brother Dupriest's stable and
contended that the circuit ought to pay him for it; claiming it as a
debt due him, because it got choked to death on the circuit by the care-
lessness of one who tied it up (probably a negro). The people told him
flatly, they would not give a cent on the score of it being a debt, but
would contribute to aid him in buying another which they did, and I believe
he got him another horse. He was very unpopular with some of the women
for his standing by them and showing how he liked this thing and that
cooked and served up. He was not very useful on the circuit, so far as
I now recollect and finally got into trouble of some sort and was expelled
from the conference.

Before I proceed further with my sketch, I desire to record a correct
list of the preachers and dates of their appointments, in that country
from 1813 to 1829. Furnished me by request recently by Rev. John C.
Jones of the Mississippi Conference, who has written the history of
Methodism in the Mississippi Country. I do this for a matter of reference,
as the former portion of this sketch was written from memory and some few
errors as to dates & c occur.

Up to 1813 and several years after the Chickasawha country was
served by the preachers sent out from the Western and South Carolina Conference to the Tombeckbee Mission and afterward a circuit. The Chickasawha
Circuit was formed in 1817. The Leaf River in 1823. Previous to this
time the Leaf River country was served, at least portions of it, partly
by the Tombeckbee preachers and partly by the Pearl River and White Sand
Circuit preachers, until an independent circuit was organized in 1823 as
above stated.

I have in another part of this sketch alluded to the missionaries
who first traversed that country; but will again allude to them in connection with those that followed them, so as to present a correct chain
in my record of the noble pioneers who opened the way, marked out the road,
sowed the seed, which by continual care and culture have developed, grown,
spread, widened and deepened into such large proportions as to cause us
to exclaim "What hath God wrought" - The following is a list in regular

49

order of the Missiona ies: In 1808 Matthew P. Sturdivant; In 1809
Michael Burge and Matt P. Sturdevant; in 1810 Michael Burge and John W.
Kennon; in 1811 John W. Kennon and John S. Ford; in 1812 William Houston
and Isaac Quinn; in 1813 I presume was the first year that a presiding
elder ever visited that country, and I will now give the names and dates
first of Presiding Elders and then the Preachers in charge. In 1813, 14,
15, & 16 Samuel Sellers, P.E. and from 1817 to 1821, Thomas Griffin, P.E..
In 1821 Chickasawha and Whitesand Circuits were included in a new District
called Alabama. From 1822 to 1824 inclusive Nicholas McIntyre, P.E. In
1825 to 1828, inclusive, Ebenezer Hearn, P.E., 1829 to 1833 James Mellard,
P.E. except that Leaf River was on the Mississippi Dist. and Thomas Griffin
P.E. in 1829.

The preachers who travelled these circuits in that country are as
follows: 1813 - Tombeckbee - Richmond Nolley, John Shrock
                    Pearl River - Samuel S. Lewis

           1814 - Tombeckbee - J. I. E. Byrd, Peter James
                    Pearl River - John Ford, Jonathan Kemp

           1815 - Tombeckbee - John S. Ford, Thomas Owens
                    Pearl River - Elijah Gentry

           1816 - Tombeckbee - Ashley Hewitt, Alex Fleming
                    Pearl River - John Menifee

           1817 - Chickasawha - Elijah Gentry
                    Pearl River - Peter James

           1818 - Chickasawha - John Booth
                    Pearl River - Wiley Ledbetter

           1819 - Chickasawha - J. I. E. Byrd
                    White Sand - Wiley Ledbetter

           1820 - Chickasawha - J. I. E. Byrd
                    White Sand - Wiley Ledbetter

           1821 - Chickasawha - Wiley Ledbetter
                    White Sand - Henry P. Cook

           1822 - Chickasawha - Thomas Owens, Edmund Pearson
                    White Sand - Wiley Ledbetter

           1823 - Chickasawha - J. I. E. Byrd, Benjamin F. Leddin
                    Leaf River - Zachariah Williams

           1824 - Chickasawha - Jonas Westerland, Joseph Calloway
                    Leaf River - Edward Harper

           1825 - Chickasawha - Edward Harper
                    Leaf River - Miles Harper

           1826 - Chickasawha - Thos. S. Abernathy, John P. Haney
                    Leaf River - Elijah B. McKay

1827 - Chickasawha - Orasmus L. Nash, Richard H. Herbert
     Leaf River - John C. Lee

1828 - Chickasawha - William H. Turnley, John W. Mann
     Leaf River - Samuel Walker

1829 - Chickasawha - Jeptha Hughs, Preston Cooper
     Leaf River - Isaac V. Enochs

1830 - Chickasawha - Richard Pipkin, Wm. Cobb
     Leaf River - to be supplied, and was by Rev. Parker

I will now also add the names of the preachers who served these circuits
until 1839.

1831 - Chickasawha - John A. Cotton, Anthony S. Dickinson
     Leaf River - James Applewhite   J. H. Mellard, P.E.

1832 - Chickasawha - Francis H. Jones, Newit Drew
     Leaf River - Samuel Graves, Enoch N. Talley   E. Hearn, P.E.

1833 - Chickasawha - Job Foster, A. C. Ramsey
     Leaf River - Newit Drew   E. Hearn, P.E.

1834 - Chickasawha - Job Foster, Ransom J. Jones
     Leaf River - D. B. Barlow, R. Crowson   E. Hearn, P.E.

1835 - Chickasawha - Theophilus Moody
     Leaf River - R. J. Jones, J. W. Holsten   E. Hearn, P.E.

1836 - Chickasawha - Thomas L. Cox
     Leaf River - A. C. Ramsey, Stephen P. Pilley E. Calloway P.E.

1837 - Chickasawha - Job Foster
     Leaf River - W. H. B. Lane from Mississippi Conference

1838 - Chickasawha - Job Foster
     Paulding - J. G. Carstarphan

Note the Leaf River circuit, or part of it, was thrown into the Mississippi
Conference by the General Conference defining a new boundary between
Mississippi and Alabama Conference, hence it lost its name and was cut up
into others in 1839. Chickasawha Circuit in 1839 was James McLeod. This
circuit had been divided also and with many others have been divided, sub-
divided, into so many pastoral charges, by adding in some places and at
different points, new territory, and building up other and new societies.
The original name and territory embraced in the old original circuits
have lost their names and identity. Yet while this is the case, and brought
about by the law of necessity, growing out of increased populations, re-
movals, deaths, and the demand for the Word of Life, in many remote corners
and sections of the country, it is a matter of gratitude to God, that the
preaching of the Gospel of Christ has been heard and received by more
persons, than otherwise would have been under the old system of large
territories as circuits.

Another cause of the dividing up, and making small pastoral charges, has grown out of the fact, a desire with all, for Sabbath preaching. The old system of preaching to the people, on week days has apparently had its day; served a good purpose when the country was new, and destitute of regular pastoral work, but now things have changed, whether for the better or not I do not say, but fear in many cases it has not proven the best for the souls of many.

I must now resume my history, which has been temporarily stopped to give the record of the different preachers on the five preceeding pages.

Our religious priviliges, as well as social, increased, grew and enlarged as time rolled on. We were regularly served with the preaching of the gospel at our school house church from the year 1824 when Uncle Ned Harper took us into his circuit, to which I have also alluded. It may be seen from the record I have made that we were favoured with the pastoral watch care, in addition to those already mentioned, of Elijah B. McKay, Samuel Walker and others whose care of the little flock and efficient preaching of the word of Life was blessed to the edification of the old, to the building up of the young converts and to the awaking of many who were in their sins; I could say many good things of those devoted men of God, and pass upon their memories many commendable eulogies, but this might be construed into a personal partiality, and doubts of the merit of such eulogies be entertained by some. Hence, I forbear saying more than they were men of God and done His work, so far as human eye could scan, or ingenuity penetrate. I must be allowed, however, to note one item of success that followed the labours of Elijah L. McKay in improving the young mind of the writer, who had been trained and brought up in the nurture and admonition of the Lord, and upon whose mind parental piety and example, had often felt the conviction "to seek the Lord while young" and"to call upon him while he was near", but would use all the means in my power to ward off this conviction and manifest as much unconcern as possible, so as to avoid the notice of others. Bro. McKays preaching fastened these impressions more indelibly on my mind and in the fall of the year I with my eldest brother, attending a Camp meeting at Salem Camp Ground on the east side of Pascagoula River, on the Chickasawha Circuit, where Bro. McKay attended. Bro. T. S. Abernathy was preacher in charge. No sooner did I get in hearing of the ground at night

52

than a thrill ran over me. Many of my old school mates I learned had
embraced religion; quite an interest had been awakened among the people.
The first sermon I heard was at 8 oclock in the morning, preached by
Bro. Abernathy from the text "acquaint now thyself with him and be at
peace thereby good shall come unto thee". This was a nail drove in a
sure place, thought the preacher knew all about me, and preached his
sermon at me. After him, Bro. McKay exhorted, which made it worse and
worse; mourners were called, but I would not go forward, nor did I until
Sunday night, when I saw and felt that some thing must be done for me
or I would be lost. I ventured forward with this feeling -"Now Lord,
if their is relief for me, I will here unwearied be till thou thy
Spirit give". About midnight thanks be unto God, the clouds dispursed,
joy and peace took possession of my poor soul and I could rejoice with
those that did rejoice and weep with those that wept. The next morning
the sun rose. O how lovely, nature seemed to put on a more beautiful
garment than ever before. Bro. Abernathy opened the door of the church,
I gave him my hand as a Methodist and now after a journey through life
of 53 years since that event, I look back and can but thank God that I
attended that camp meeting and that I joined the church that lovely
morning. I have never regretted it, nor have I ever doubted that a
change of some kind passed upon my poor heart, that blessed Sabbath
night. I have had doubts of my progress, and of doing my whole duty,
but never doubted that God did not bless me then and there.

- Social and Educational Priviliges -

The country although sparsely settled up, compared with other sections
yet sufficient to afford neighbors, schools and other preaching places,
up and down Red Creek and Black Creek so that as years passed by the
preachers faced other appointments, organized other societies and quite
an improvement in a social as well as religious sense. Our own immediate
neighborhood was somewhat enlarged by the acquisition of old Uncle Jesse
Graves and his wife, although no children and he blind, yet he was a
good neighbor, pious and added, what time he remained there, two good
members to the church. In addition to these Bro. Ezekiel Cowart with
a large family of children settled the place formerly owned by Solomon
Dearmon, which was quite an accession in point of social, religious and
educational priviliges.

About eight miles above us, another neighborhood was finally formed

of all Methodist, at least the first settlers, consisting of Rev. James
Ford, Edmund Hester, Thomas Evans, James Evans, David Evans, and Mr.
Dozier, all from White Sand in Lawrence County, Mississippi. Subsequently,
Col. Bond, William Bond, Brantly Bond, Elisha Bond, Seth Batson and others
settled in and contiguous to that neighborhood. These last were mostly,
if not all, adherents of the Baptist denomination. This formed quite
an excellent community of good, industrious, sober and honest citizens,
so that very soon, a preaching place was procured, and they were in-
corporated into the Leaf River Circuit by Br. Miles Harper, in 1825, and
was attended annually by the preachers thereafter; and in 1831 under the
ministry of Bro. James Applewhite who had with him at the time, three
young candidates for the Itinerant work, viz: Charles J. Carney; Absalom
Cavin, and Theophilus Moody, a good revival of religion occured in that
community, and several were converted and added to the church.

Above this neighborhood, about ten or twelve miles, possibly, was
another excellent community, made up of such men, and their families;
James Denmark, John Dale; James Tillman, Resters, Lees and others, all
of the Baptist persuasion and in the midst of which, a Baptist Church
was built, and quite a large membership organized, where there was
stated monthly preaching by the ministers of that denomination, which I
believe is still kept up at that place or at least in that neighborhood.

I have now shown the settling up of that pine woods country, north
west of where we lived and a portion of the last neighborhood referred
to was settled before our move there in 1820.

I must now in the same connection, refer to communities east and
south east of us. Near the mouth of Red and Black Creek and stretching
down to the Pascagoula River to what was called Brewers Bluff, which
place was for awhile the county site of Jackson County. There lived a
fine community, tolerably thickly settled up, with and enterprising
people, so that good schools for that time and that day were not uncommon;
and where finally some few churches and church houses were organized and
built.

Among the many composing these communities, were a few of the following viz: Joseph Rodgers, Frederic Rodgers, Jesse Rodgers, James Bradley;
James Dannelly; Carter; John Brewer; John Mounger; the Wares; Henry Brown;
the Johnsons and many others. And since then, John McDonald, Capt. Snell

54

Mr. Walker, John Havens, Mr. Dwire, Rev. Henry Fletcher, and others. The most if not all the first settlers in this community moved off at an early date to Hinds County, MS, but their places were filled by others.

Having now shown up and described the communities and our associations with them, and affording much social intercourse and enjoyment to us, I must now cross the River, and say some thing, of the excellent moral, sober and religious communities on the east side, particularly of those making up and surrounding the neighborhood of Salem Camp Ground. And let it be borne in mind, that the social and religious enjoyments of that day and time were not confined to the immediate neighborhoods surrounding us, but spread out and extended over a large area of country embracing neighborhoods, communities and churches from five to thirty miles. It was no uncommon thing for persons, particularly the young to attend Quarterly Meetings, Camp Meetings, Singing Schools, Marriages and Festivals as remote from them at a distance of twenty five and thirty miles.

The same may be said of the older ones, in their attendance upon religious convocations and services.

Hence Salem Camp Meeting was a place of annual resort, by young and old, a distance of thirty miles from where we lived, and not unfrequently tenters from our community pitched their tents there and assisted in supporting the large crowds that attended upon these occasions.

This camp ground was established in 1826, the year Rev. T. S. Abernathy and John Haney traveled the Chickasawha circuit and the next year or the year following probably when Rev. W. N. Tumley was in charge a fine arbor was erected, in front of and only a short distance from the church house, both of which were finally destroyed by fire. But the good people, nothing daunted, set to work built a new church, a new arbor, moved or built new tents, about one mile, from the original one, and kept up continuously an annual camp meeting ever since, with probably one or two omissions, and these from unavoidable obstacles. Where is the community that can show such devotion to the cause of God, to the building up and keeping in working order the machinery of the church, the spiritual development and growth of her members, the conviction and conversion of the hundreds who sought and obtained peace and pardon on that Camp Ground; and from which many, yea very many, have crossed over the stream of death

55

and pitched their tents on the other shore. Where are now the original tenters, that first inaugerated the plan and carried out to successful development, the object and aim of this camp ground? Echo answered where? They have left for their reward, but thanks be unto God, "the mantle of the old Elijah's have fallen over the young Elishas" who manfully have gathered up the armor and wore it in triumph, and carrying out the plans and performing the work left by their venerable ancestors.

Where is the sainted Peter Helverston, William Carter, Matthew Carter, Samuel Davis, Henry Fletcher, Edmund Goff, Bryant Ferrell, William Mizzle, Father Wells, Isaac Wells, beside many others who were generally seen on that ground with open arms, open hearts, and open tents to receive, feed, and care for the people assembled there to hear the Word of Life. A few may yet linger here, but the most, if not all, have gone, and we indulge the blessed hope – gone to the Good World.

But must I in giving these notes, pass by the good sisters of that community who were not only help mates, in these great religious efforts of moral and religious reform, but were in a great measure the more active and successful agents in the accomplishment of the great good effected; not only in preparing and serving with a lavish hand such viands as were needful for the body, but more especially in instructing, advising, encouraging and praying for the sin sick, and broken hearted; and by their many joyful shouts of praise to God, gave evidence, that they felt what they said and enjoyed what they felt, giving unmistakeable evidence that they had been with Jesus. I must here refer to some of them, to whose kindness and care were shown me, together with their husbands and brethern generally, I feel greatly indebted, not only at the several camp meetings I attended there, but likewise while I was among them as junior preacher on that circuit in 1833. Viz: Sister Helverston, the two Sister Carters, Sister Davis, the two sister Goffs, Sister Ferrell, Sister Wells and Sister Fletcher, and many other matrons, whose pious labors and efforts done much in advancing and building up the church around them. Some few of these are still here, watching and waiting for God to announce to "come up higher". The others have fought the fight through and no doubt obtained a crown. In this connection I must not omit to mention some of the younger members of that church especially the female portion, whose piety, as evidenced by constant walking with God, their secret, and family devotions, frequently in their fathers family, their labours and public

Editor's Notes:

Page 49 - Old Brother Dupriest's stable - This is Dupree rather than
Dupriest, since the Dupriest family had not yet moved to this area.
They were still located in Washington County, AL and Wayne and Jones
County, MS.

Page 49, 50, and 51 - Biographical sketches of these preachers listed
can be found in The History of Methodism in Mississippi by Jones and
The History of Methodism in Alabama by Lazenby

Page 53 - Uncle Jesse Graves appears in the 1820 Census of Jackson County,
MS.

Ezekiel Cowart and his wife, Margaret Cochran Cowart have been referred
to previously in the Editor's Notes. In 1820 Ezekiel and Margaret
Cowart had 3 sons and 5 daughters at home. Some of their children were
already grown and married. By 1830 Ezekiel Cowart and his family had
moved to Greene County, MS where he lived the remainder of his long
life. Ezekiel served in the War of 1812 in the Mississippi Militia
and received a pension for this service.

Page 54 - Community formed 8 miles above the Ramsey place consisting
mostly of people from Lawrence County. James Ford, Edmund Hester,
Thomas Evans, James Evans can all be found in the 1820 census of
Lawrence County. Thomas Evans has 3 males in his household age 26-45.
One of these is probably a brother David who moved to Jackson County
with him. Mr. Dozier is not found in Lawrence County in 1820 nor
elsewhere in Mississippi. He apparently did not remain in Jackson
County for he is not there in 1830. These people do not appear on
the 1825 State Census of Jackson County, so their arrival was between
1825 and 1830.

Col. Bond, William Bond, Brantly Bond, Elisha Bond, Seth Batson and
others settled in and contiguous to that neighborhood. These settlers
with the exception of Seth Batson came from Lawrence and Covington
Counties, MS. Seth Batson had been living in Hancock County in 1820.

Above this neighborhood, about ten or twelve miles was another excellent
Community made up of . . . James Denmark was living in Hancock County,
MS in 1820; John Dale does not appear in Misssissippi in 1820; James
Tillman is already in Jackson County in 1820; Rester family is that of
Frederick Rester (R.S.); Lee family is that of Uriah Lee.

This migration to Jackson County after 1820 must have some connection
with the opening of the Federal Land Office at Augusta in 1822 and
the appointment of 2 representative to handle land sales in the Jackson
County area.

Brewer's Bluff - John Brewer's land was in section 1, Township 5S, Range
7W. The location of Brewer's Bluff on the Pascagoula and the county
site of Jackson County at one time. John Brewer was earlier in Washington
County, M.T. where he can be found buying and selling land. Susanna
Brewer of Washington County, M.T. is probably his mother and George
Brewer of that place, his brother.

Editor's Notes:

Page 54 - Joseph Rogers was from South Carolina. He was a steamboat pilot on the Mississippi Sound and was married to Nancy Holden. A son Joseph Griffin Rogers who was born May 8, 1812 at Red Creek, Jackson County, MS served in the state legislature in 1911 as a state representative.

James Bradley is found on the census of Jackson County in 1820, but no land record was found for him at that time.

Nicholas and William Dannelly are found on the 1820 census of Jackson County, MS but no James.

Carter family - This family is well written about and documented in Four Centuries on the Pascagoula by Cyril Cain.

John Mounger and William Mounger are found on the Jackson County 1820 Census but no land records were found for them at that time.

James Ware was an early settler from Ireland. He had applied for a Spanish Land Grant and stated that he had a wife and seven children in 1817.

Henry Brown was listed in Lawrence County, MS in 1820 census.

Minor W. Johnson was living in Jackson County as early as 1812.

John McDonald is not identified. There are three in Mississippi in 1820 - one in Perry County, One in Wayne County, and one in Greene County.

Capt. Snell is Samuel Snell listed as owning land on the south side of Smith Creek in 1818.

Page 55 - Mr. Walker - Charles Walker appears on the 1830 Census of Jackson County, MS

John Havens came to the area prior to 1816 and settled near Red Hill Church. He was from Virginia and his wife was Susan Flurry.

Mr. Dwire - Daniel Dwire was listed in the 1820 census of Jackson County.

Rev. Henry Fletcher came from the Carolinas around 1817. He had land on Indian Fork Creek in 1818. His wife was Elizabeth Goff. He was active in organizing Red Hill Church.

Page 56 - Peter Helveston lived in what is now George County, MS. Many descendants are buried in cemeteries in the Basin area of George County. An early land record was not found for him

William Carter and Matthew Carter are well presented and documented in 4 Centuries on the Pascagoula by Cyril Cain. Early land records show Matthew Carter living on the Pascagoula River in Section 18, Township 4, Range 6W and William Carter living on the River in Section 37, Township 4, Range 7W. Date of the land claims for both is 1811.

Editor's Notes:

Page 56 - Samuel Davis was living on the Pascagoula River in Section 9, Township 3, Range 7 in 1812.

Edmund Goff - Edmund Goff came early to Jackson County along with his father and others of his family. His wife was Lucretia Wells. He had land in Section 27, Township 4, Range 6 and in Section 30, township township 3, Range 6W in 1812.

Bryant Ferrell settled in Jackson County, MS in 1812 coming here from Screvin County, Georgia. The Ferrill Cemetery in George County, MS still exists today where Bryant Ferrill is buried. See article on Ferrill Family in Jackson County Genealogical Society Journal, Vol. 2, no. 4 for more complete information on this family.

William Mizzle is William Mizell. The Mizells were relatives of the Carters. The Mizell family appears in detail in Four Centuries on the Pascagoula by Cyril Cain

Father Wells is Henry Wells who had land on the Pascagoula River in 1812.

prayers at the church whenever called on gave them the character of the mostmost devoted and exemplary members of the church in all that country. I refer particularly to the four Miss Carter's; Sabra, Cassie, Nancy and Susan. Others in the same community were entitled no doubt to equal eulogies with these and I do not mean to draw any invidious distinctions, but refer to these as example of female piety.

These young sisters were continually model young Christians such as are rarely seen especially in this day. Two of them I believe still remain, and the other two gone the way of all the earth and no doubt gone to heaven. But while these and many others have passed away, others have risen up and taken their places. "God may, and does often, destroy the workmen, but still carry on the work"

It would be I presume, a useless task, one that could not now be performed, to form any correct estimate of the number of persons who have embraced religion at that Camp Ground. For I suppose their name is "Legion". Some may have made ship wreck of the faith and turned like the sow that was washed to her wallowing in the mire, yet hundreds no doubt have proved faithful and some long since gone to their reward; while others are still here labouring, toiling and watching to be ready to go and join those who are gone before. "The little leven" that was put in the three measures of meal leavened the whole lump. So the seeds of grace scattered here in the hearts of many have permeated and diffused itself to such an extent, so as not only to save the souls of its recipients but have been diffused and scattered in other communities so that the fruits and effects of the sowing the seed of the Kingdom at Salem, may be seen and will finally be gathered in distant fields, where it has been deposited by these upon whose hearts it was first sown at old Salem. Witness the many young men who were converted there and have gone forth as ministers of the Gospel, scattering the good seed from east to west, north to south. Besides these, look at the numbers who have filled lower offices in the church, such as class leaders, local preachers, exhorters, stewards and Sunday School Superintendants, who in their sphere, are as important in doing the great work of evangelizing and Christianizing the world as those who occupy a higher position in the work. From these various sowers, and working agencies, what may we expect, at the Great Harvest? When God shall come to gather into the Heavenly Garner the sheaves of the Kingdom? They will come from the east, from the west,

60

from the north and from the south saying we went forth sowing in tears,
but we return bringing many sheaves with us. And, O, will not the good
people of Salem and throughout south eastern Mississippi come up there
for a share in that great Harvest. God grant that you and I may be there
and receive a welcome to the banquet of our blessed Lord.

Having now given an extended account of our church privileges, and
sources of social intercourse and enjoyments, I must now return to our
Red Creek home and note, some of few items of domestic improvement and
educational facilities. Our farm was opened gradually every year until
finally we had for that country a respectable place. Improvements were
added annually, as we got able to do the necessary work, so that in a
few years we made provisions sufficient for home consumption. The two
or three first years were the most labourous and hard ones in making
a living, but our stock of cattle and hogs done well, increased rapidly,
and by the sale of beef cattle and some pork every year, taking to market
butter, chickens, eggs, peltry, venison hams, wild turkeys occasionally
killed in the woods, by which means many of the luxuries and necessities
of life were supplied. Our labour force likewise increased. .Brother
William and Daniel, who were small, and not large enough to do heavy work
when we first settled there, yet of considerable help even then; in clearing off the rubbish, piling brush, making fence, attending the stock & c
and making themselves useful in many ways, grew up and soon became efficient
hands in any and every kind of manual labour necessary to be done; and,
finally, before Father and Mother's deaths were the dependants of the
family.

The first school we had in this neighborhood was taught by an
Irishman named Donaho; a near sighted man, whose school continued only
for three months. Father and Mr. Holder were the only patrons. He was
a good scholar and a good teacher and taught at a house one and a half
miles from us which had been built by a man by the name of McDuffee who
(if I do not mistake) married Miss Nancy Holland. This man did not
settle this place, and afterwards died. This place was afterwards
occupied by old Bro. Jesse Craves, to whom allusion has already been
made. And here at this place a Camp Meeting was held in 1831 when
Bro. James Applewhite was on the circuit, and Bro. James Millard was
the Presiding Elder.

61

The next school was taught by Samuel W. Francis at the half way
school house between Bro. Holders and Fathers to which also allusion
has been made, as answering the double purpose of school house and
church. Mr. Francis was a fine teacher, a Virginian, taught here six
months, gave us all a fine start, advanced his pupils rapidly; a fine
scribe and under his instructions I learned to write. After this school
was out, he moved to Thomas Bilbo's on the river and taught there for
some time. My father sent me to him six months more and boarded me
with him. He had now married Miss Rebecca Longino. Before this however
Father sent Bro. Andrew and me to Mr. Berry on the river, not far from
Brewer's Bluff (now Dwire's) and boarded us with a James Bradley. Here
we associated with the boys and girls of a thickly settled neighborhood
viz the Moungers, Carters, Brewers, Rodgers and others. This school
however was like the most of the schools in that day a three months
school. From what I can now recollect, I don't think we derived much
profit from the little instructions we received here.

The next school in our neighborhood was taught by the writer of
these sketches. Having had some better advantages in point of education
than any member of Fathers family, and having advanced, in some of the
English branches beyond any of my age in the community, and especially
by my twelve months with Mr. Francis, it was insisted upon my taking the
school there for a time at least, so I reluctantly consented. A new
school house was soon put up, not far from Holders Ferry on Red Creek
so as to put it in reach of Ezekiel Cowarts on the north side of the
creek. So the time of opening was announced; the young inexperienced
teacher was on hand at the time appointed; took a list of the pupils
who presented themselves at this new institution of learning when he
found that there were four from Cowart's, five from Holders and four
from Fathers, the majority larger and some older than myself - young
men and young ladies grown. My heart beat faster than usual, the
responsibility was heavy, I really dreaded the undertaking. To manage
and control this school was a matter of no little concern, being my
own school mates, play mates, brothers and sisters, besides the fear of
insubordination to my authority, rendered the situation anything but
pleasant. But having taken hold nothing remained for me now but to
make the trial and go ahead. I assumed command, put them to work, and
very soon the scare was off, and I had a pleasant time, with some few
exceptions. All appeared to labour and study to improve, and were

generally submissive and obedient to my authority. This being my first,
I contracted rather a taste for teaching and followed it for several
years afterwards at intervals.

    - Other Schools which I and Brother Andrew Attended -

My opportunities were somewhat superior to any other member of the
family. Bro. Andrew went to a Mr. John James who taught in Greene
County near Leakesville, in the neighborhood of McRaes and Martins, to
which community I have already referred. James was an Irishman and fine
teacher and afterwards he taught in Washington County, Alabama in the
neighborhood of William Godfreys, here brother Andrew went to him another
session. I had the advantages of one session with Mr. Norman McLeod who
taught at Thomas Bilbos and subsequently, in 1829, I spent a few months
in school on the Bay at John McRaes where I sutdied more correctly English
Grammar, bookkeeping and geography under the tuition of a Mr. Morrison,
an excellent teacher; and after I left this school took a school and
taught several months, in Thomas Bilbo's neighborhood. Previous to
this, and before I went to this last school, and afterward, I taught
several schools in different portions of the country. One more in
Father's neighborhood, two in the neighborhood of Thomas Evans; one in
Mr. Denmark and Dale community; one in Copiah County, and the last one
I ever taught was in 1830 and 31 for Judge John and Peter Fairley. By
pursuing this course of teaching I improved my little education as much
as if I had been taught in school, and also would make a little to aid
me in the last two schools I have mentioned.

Father had a small legacy left him by his Father who died in
Bedford County, Tennessee. He empowered brother Andrew and sent him
after it; but when he got there had some difficulty in getting it from
the Executor or Administrator, and rather than stay there and be
compelled to wait on expenses; compromised by taking a part in horses
and a part in money; fifty dollars of which proved to be counterfiet
which he entirely lost. The two horses he brought home turned out
well.

Note: The preceeding part of this sketch was written during the summer
of 1879. The following commencing on the next page, summer of 1880
most part in the month of August.

Editor's Notes:

Page 61 – Mr. Donaho, school teacher. Unidentifed. There were no
Donaho families listed on the Jackson County, MS census during this
time. The only families by that surname in Mississippi in 1820 are
in Pike and Jefferson counties.

Page 61 – a man named McDuffie. Probably Allen McDuffey who is a
young man age 16-26 in 1820 with a wife age 10-16. Allen McDuffey
does not show up again on the Mississippi Census and is gone by
the 1825 State Census. However, the widow Agnes McDuffie does
appear in the 1825 State Census.

Page 61 – Miss Nancy Holland – Nancy Agnes Holland daughter of
Charles Holland, Revolutionary Soldier, and his wife Sarah Hughes.
After the death of Allen McDuffey she married John Richard Byrd.
This information from the Obituary of John Richard Byrd written
by J. H. Hollarnd and appearing in the March 11, 1186 issue of
the New Orleans Christian Advocate and the March 19, 1886 issue
of the Pascagoula Democrat Star, and Holland information supplied
by Don Davis, 5013 Magnolia St., Moss Point, MS 39563

Page 62 – Samuel W. Francis married Rebecca Longino who is probably
a sister of John Thomas Longino, Jr. who married A. C. Ramsey's sister.
The Longino family appears on the census of Lawrence County in 1820.

Page 62 – Mr. Berry – possibly David Berry who came to Mississippi
with the Fairleys.

Page 62 – Families mentioned attending school at Mr. Berry's on the
river. See previous notes on these families.

Page 63 – Mr. John James, Greene County, MS and Washington County,
AL – Johnathan James listed on the 1811 Tax Roll of Washington
County, M.T. The James family was found early at the Choctaw Trading
Post, St. Stephens, M.T. (AL) and migrated into Greene County, MS.
Oldest member of this family Phillip James, Sr.

Page 63 – William Godfrey of Washington County, AL. William
Godfrey first appears on the 1813 Tax Roll of Washington County, M.T.
an owning 271 acres on Hickory Level which was purchased from the
U.S. Government. He had 20 slaves.

Page 63 – on the Bay at John McRaes – John McRae is buried south of
Gautier, MS in Jackson County. He died in 1835.

Page 63 – Mr. Morrison. The only Morrison found in Jackson County,
MS at this time period is John D. Morrison.

Page 63 – Norman McLeod from North Carolina lived in Greene County, MS
in the southern part. He was born ca 1800 and married Millicent R.
Dantzler. Norman McLeod had a son Rufus who married Elizabeth Ramsey
and a son Calvin H. who married Susan Ramsey.

1825

Marriage of my sister Ann.

This event occured August the 4th 1825, when she formed an alliance with John R. Longino of Lawrence County, Mississippi. A gentleman of fine moral habits and their union was a happy one. They settled on Crooked Creek in said county, where they resided until 1827 when they removed and settled near us on Red Creek, where they remained until after Father's death. And then went back to Lawrence and spent their lives there, raising a large family of children who are now in that country at and around the old homestead and doing well; respectable and useful citizens and members of the Baptist Church mostly. Their oldest son moved to Missouri, the only one of the eleven children outside of Lawrence County who are alive. Augustus died during the war, John T. was killed at Franklin, Tennessee.

Brother and sister Longino were both members of the Methodist Chruch wile they lived near us on Red Creek and for several years after they returned to Lawrence; but being cut off almost entirely from church pirvileges in that communion, and being surrounded by and associated mostly with large churches, and communities of the Baptist denomination, they united with that church, and lived and died acceptable members thereof testifying at the last their readiness to depart.

In the fall of 1825 after sisters marriage and settlement in Lawrence I visited them in search of a school, whcih I obtained in Copiah County, in the neighborhood of Isaac Ryan, Soloman Dearman and John McCraney on Long Creek four miles north of Gallatin, the county site of said county. Here I taught unti the Spring of 1826 when I desired to return home; but having sold my horse, I at first saw no way to accomplish it, without buying another. But fortunately or unfortunately for me (as the sequal will show) Mr. John B. Short, had come to that county from near my Father's neighborhood, riding an Indian pony and wished to send it back and offered me the poney, provided I would deliver him to his friends at home; to which I readily consented, got ready and started. At the end of the first days travel, I was at my borther-in-laws in Lawrence, where I intended to spend a few days; and having that day crossed the Pearl River, where the Indian trail crosses from the Six Towns (Choctaw nation) to Natches and where no doubt the pony had been before, and knew it, gave me trouble.

65

Being fine grazing around where my brother in law lived, I turned
him out footloose with his horses. In the evening he was missing, but
being shod on the fore feet, which was uncommon there, I started in pur-
suit tracked him back to where I crossed the river. He took the trail
a straight chute for Six Towns, his old home no doubt. I pursued him
into Simpson County where I lost his tract and finally gave up the chase
and returned. Now what to do, I did not know; about a hundred miles from
home, young and scarry; not much money and the man's pony gone to the
Indians, who would conceal him if pursued and found; and I would have to
pay for him. These reflections rendered my situation unpleasant and
annoying, but as the Psalmist says "Mourning may endure for the night,
but joy comethin in the morning." And so it turned out.

I hired myself to work in the farm with James Kirby, who kept the
ferry on the river where I and the pony corssed; the first and only time
I ever hired to do manual labour. Indians were crossing there almost
daily going to or from Natchez, and I now became the principal ferryman
and by the suggestion of Mr. Kirby, I hired several Indians to look up
and bring the pony, but had but little confidence in their ever returning
the horse provided they found him. The last one I contracted with was
a good looking old fellow, better dressed than any of the others. I
described the horse by taking him to the stable and pointing out by another
horse all the marks of the pony, particularly his shoes. "Yea" me find
him", "me fetch in half moon," two weeks. How much you charge me? Four
dollar; all right Bobashila, Chickamawfand. I give you four dollars. So
we parted, and at the end of two weeks, to my surprise, and great gratification the honest old Indian brought me my horse; fat and sleek as a mole;
had walked and led him by a rope the entire way. You may well imagine
my feelings now. I offered him paper money, but nau! nau! was his reply
wanted silver. Had to go off a mile to ask Brooks to get the change, who
kept the whiskey to sell; got the silver and a bottle of whiskey for the
good old fellow; and in the mean time Mrs. Kirby had given him an old dog
that she wanted to get rid of, and when I paid him off and gave him the
liquor, he took a dram and drank to our health, I suppose, in Choctaw
language; got his dinner and left the happiest man I have seen for years
tidding us all good by, shaking our hands, and saying "Bobashila! Bobashila!
Chickamawfana " & c.

A short time after this my mother and brother Andrew came up to

Lawrence on a visit to sisters and brother Andrew took the pony back to
Mr. Short, and I got rid of him,much to the joy of my heart.

I then returned home with them, and the fall of that year 1826 I
attended the Camp Meeting at Salem Camp, where I have never regretted.
And now after fifty four years have passed by, I can but thank God that
I, then and there, gave my heart and since, consecrated my life to His
service.

In 1826 as stated elsewhere Elijah B. McKay travelled our circuit,
Leaf River. In 1827 John G. Lee and 1828 Samuel Walker.

But by some conflicting arrangements, our little church was, for
a while, left out, or for want of time could not be attended particularly
in 1827 by Brother Lee, who had an appointment on Black Creek at Mr.
Zean Wilsons, but gave us his services once or twice at night, at Bro.
Holder's house. This temporary arrangement was over come the next year
by Bro. Walker who preached regularly at our School House on Little Creek
once every four weeks, in 1828. In 1829, we were blessed with the services
of Bro. Isaac V. Enocks who like those who preceeded him, was acceptable,
prompt, and useful, a good preacher, and energetic in acquiring knowledge.
If my memory serves me correctly, he was then either learning or reviewing
English Grammar. Being with him frequently, he and I had several pleasant
moments looking into old Murray, who was at that day and time, the standard
on English Grammar.

One incident occured, while accompanying him from our neighborhood
to his next appointment at Bilbo's church, and I think it was on his
first round on the circuit; at any rate it was winter and a very cold day.
When we got to Black Creek at Lewis Parker's ferry as it was called, where
every man was his own ferryman, and required to leave the ferry boat or
flat on one side and the skiff or batteau on the other, so that none coming
or going either way would be disappointed in getting one or the other,
but on this occasion some one had disregarded the rule, and both were on
the opposite side and the creek was swollen and the weather cold. The
preacher anxious to get to his appointment that day about five miles
distant, and now completely cut off. In casing about, I told him if we
could make a raft that would bear me up, and launch it some distance above
the ferry, I thought I could so steer it as to strike the opposite bank
some where so that I could get to the flat. This struck his fancy, only
was afraid I might fail, or take cramp, or make me sick. I told him I

was a good swimmer and if I got off I could swim out & c. So we went
to work, found several light pine logs fallen recently, broken up into
proper lengths, looked around and got grapevines and tied vines enough,
and very soon had our craft in launching order. I was about shucking myself, divesting all my clothing, had already put the raft in and would
soon have made the trial in home made navigation, when lo! and behold!
we heard some one hallo at the ferry where the flat was. This was a
relief to us both and particularly to me. It proved to be Mr. John
McRae who lived at the bay, and was returning home from a trip up the
country and had to come that way to get across Black Creek. Hence I
regarded this as a Providence, and the preacher filled his appointment.

My brother Andrew was married this year, July 2d to Miss Nancy Holder
and settled a new place about one mile from brother Holders and at which
place Daniel Walker, now 1880, lives. Here he remained for a few years
and then moved about four miles south on the main road leading to the
coast, where he done well; but had the misfortune to lose his wife, who
had borne him five children. He subsequently married Miss Caroline Evans
who before his death was the mother of thirteen children.

He represented his county in the Legislature one or two terms and
one in the Senate, and also filled the office of Judge of Probate for
one term, probably more.

His family of children increasing so rapidly, and growing up, and
school facilities being so meager, in that thinly populated country, and
entertaining an ambition to educate his children, he removed to Greene
County to Salem High School where he intended to remain until his older
children, at least, had the advantage of an education, but alas! God ordered it otherwise. He took the typhoid fever and died and was buried
there by the Masonic Fraternity, of which order he was a member. In 1830
he and his wife both joined the Methodist E. Church and lived and died in
that church. Three of his sons were lost in the war. Alfred by disease.
Abiezer who commanded a company was killed at Atlanta. Daniel was killed
at Franklin Tennessee in the battle. The remaining 15 are still living.
In 1830 the Leaf River circuit was left by the conference without a
preacher, to be supplied, which was done by a Bro. Parker, a bachelor,
an ordinary preacher, but a good man, and done all he could to build up
and strengthen the church, but no marked success followed.

During this year I had to attend (1830) as a witness for the State against Thomas Bilbo, for an assault and battery, on the person of Wyatt Dupree, his son-in-law, and which occured the year before at Bilbo's house, while I was engaged there teaching school. The causes of the affray were such that it was considered by the jury almost justifiable; and therefore imposed on the defendant a mere nominal fine of five dollars only.

It may not be amiss to give here some of the circumstances of this tragical scene, for certainly it was a scene of that character. Mr. Dupree had married Maj. Bilbo's second daughter, Jane, who at that time had borne him one child; and had lived on the Major's place for some time after their marriage; during which he had debauched the eldest daughter, Nancy, sister of his wife; and who had that year 1829 given birth to a child. In the mean time Dupree had moved to Greene County, the neighborhood of his father. When I first went there to take charge of my school, Miss Nancy was there in the family; but I could but notice, in her movements, and associations that something was wrong; and soon after was sent off to W. R. Bilbo, the Major's brother, who subsequently divulged the whole affair to me. Some little time after this, Dupree and his wife, paid the Major a visit, came there on Friday morning and it was supposed, intended to stay until after Sunday. Friday evening however, he went to W. R. Bilbos, I suppose to ascertain the true condition of affairs, came back, and Saturday morning went home, giving as an excuse, that he wished to attend church at home on Sunday, as their pastor would preach there that day. Dupree was a member of the church, and I believe class leader. He did attend and withdrew from the church on that day, which he ought to have done long before this.

Some time after this, Dupree, wife and child came down to the Majors and halloed at the ferry to get across. Major Bilbo's place was on a high, beautiful, elevated bluff and a ferry kept at the river, about one quarter of a mile from his house; sufficiently near to hear the signal of persons wishing to cross over. The Major heard the signal, and through a negro he learned that it was Wyatt Dupree and family. He, accordingly, dispatched a negro man to ferry him over while he was making arrangements for his reception, which consisted in gathering together his fire arms, sword cane & c and placing them in one room where they would be hidden from the eye of Dupree, whom he invited into the other room. The house consisted of two rooms with a passage between. My school house was situated about one quarter of a mile from the residence at the south side of

an old field which had not been cultivated for a long time, except a portion west of the path leading to the school house, but did not obstruct
my view of the house; could discern plainly persons or objects moving about
at the house, also the portion of the field in cultivation. On this particular morning, I saw Maj. Bilbo walking very hurriedly up the school path,
crossed over the fence where he had several hands picking peas; very soon
returned followed by two negro men, Ned and Ben. Jack was at the house
and who had been sent to ferry over Dupree and family. Soon after this
I heard the report of a gun, which from the sound appeared to be in the
house. I asked his sons, Joseph and William "what that meant"?, they
replied "they supposed father had shot a hawk". In a very short time I
saw a little negro coming at full speed, crying out "Master had shot
Mass Wyatt". This alarming news could but fill us all with consternation
and not wishing to witness the scene, I did not go. Neither did William.
Joseph went and directly another messenger from the Major himself, saying
"dismiss school and come immediately", which I did.

On arriving at the place, I was met by Mrs. Bilbo in the yard, perfectly frantic, ringing her hands and in deep distress. "Well" says she,
"we've had a battle" and commenced giving me the details, but remarked
"go in and you will learn all about it". And so I did and such a scene
I had never witnessed before. Dupree was tied hard and fast, the cords
binding his hands were passed around and under his legs; he seated in a
low chair, his wife by his side, the lower part of one ear nearly cut
off by a severe punch of the muzzle of an old double barrel shot gun;
the blood running from his ear and Jo Bilbo standing by guarding him
with a double shot gun. Outside of the house on a blanket, lay Ned, one
of the negroes brought from the pea field, shot through the chest with
a load of buckshot, groaning and in a dying condition. Jo, the guard,
remarked to me, "If he (Dupree)moved a step he would shoot him." I
told him to put up his gun, I thought there had been shooting enough
done. Dupree remarked "I am not going to move, I couldn't if I wanted
to, and would not if I could". Previous to this as he told me afterwards,
he had fears of their taking his life, but said after you got there those
fears left me, and I never was more rejoiced to see you come.

The Major commenced giving me in detail the circumstances of the
case, when Dupree stopped him, and gave his account of it. From both of
whom, I learned the following facts. Dupree did not intend to stop, but
when he rode up to the gate, intending to leave his wife and child, and

change horses as he was going down the river to see Mr. Devise, a mill wright, to get him to work on his father's mill. Maj. Bilbo met them and insisted so strongly on Dupree's stopping and going in that he, Dupree, finally yielded to his earnest solicitations, thinking it true friendship and respect, that prompted the manifested the anxiety on the part of the Major. So into the house they went, the Major leading the way with the child in his arms. When they entered the house, they were conducted into the Major's room, chairs were placed for them, not far from the door, the Major stepped out and placed two negro men in the passage, one on each side of the door to catch Dupree if he should attempt to escape and to assist in confining him; whereupon the Major approached the door with a double shot gun cocked, and remarked, "now you rascal, if you move I will shoot you or blow your brains out."

Dupree being very irritable and withall sprightly sprang at the door, and being left handed knocked the gun with his left hand which fired and emptied the whole load into the chest of poor Ned. And still pursuing and following up his attack, backed the Major across the passage into the door of the other room, which when he entered, and Dupree reaching after him with his left hand, his head turned to the right, the Major gave him such a severe punch with the muzzle of the gun, which came in contact with his ear and that side of the head that it knocked him down, and so stunned him, as to lose the power of resistance any further, whereupon Bilbo and his negroes tied him and had him bound in the condition I found him.

I asked Maj. Bilbo what he intended to do with him. His reply was "I intended to tie him, take him back over the river, give him a hundred lashes and send him home. Whereupon Dupree remarked "if you had it would have been the last one you would have ever troubled." And no doubt it would have been, for he was of fearless, courageous stock and would have resented such an insult at the peril of his life, or the life of the assailant.

~ The Sequel To This Tradegdy ~

Maj. Bilbo now wished for some one to go after the magistrate, Allen McLendon, Esq. and also wished Judge John Fairley. I volunteered my services. Ned was not yet dead. In the evening I returned with the Squire and the Judge. The negro was now dead. Hence arrangements for a jury of inquest was now in order. The constable Mr. Tucker had come, unto whom the Major had delivered up the prisoner, and who had loosed the cords from

71

his hands, but had his arms tightly tied around his body. Squire
McLendon asked for the charges against Dupree, and what he intended to
do in the case. Bilbo replied the charge was murder, and he wished him
prosecuted for killing the negro. And after hearing the testimony on
both sides, and all the particulars, the Squire remarked I find no
charge against this man and consequently shall release him, which he did.
The next day an inquest was held and verdict rendered according to the
facts. At the close of this inquest, a strong effort was made by friends
and citizens to bring about a reconciliation between these parties, so as
to drop any further legal proceedings on the part of Dupree aginst Bilbo,
for the investigation had brought out clearly that Bilbo instead of
Dupree was the agressor; and that he had become liable to Dupree for
damages besides subjected himself to a prosecution of assault and battery
with an intent to kill. These influences were effectual on Dupree, who
waived suit for damages; and promised he would not prosecute provided he
was not forced to do so by the Solicitor and Grand Jury, which he was and
the case was tried and verdict rendered as before stated. There were
four lawyers engaged in the case — Col. Morris (commonly called Coon Morris)
Col. Sterling for the State, and Col. Alsberry and Col. Damevon (Dameron)
for the Defendant, all of whom acquitted themselves with credit for and
against the allegations involved. Col. Alsberry's speech, as well as I
now recollect, had a telling effect on the minds of the jury. Hence the
light fine imposed.

— Reminiscences of 1831 —

During this year, a general revival of religion prevailed on the
Leaf River Circuit under the ministry of Bro. James Applewhite who had
been appointed by the Annual Conference preacher in charge. Having in-
cidentally alluded on page 74 to a portion of this years work by the Godly
man in connection with his corps of young men whom he had under training
for the itinerant work vis: Carney, Gavin, Moody. I shall only state
here, more in detail, the character of the work, the energy with which it
was prosecuted and devotion to duty of those who had it in charge.

Brother Applewhite was what may be properly termed a revivalist.
While his talent for doctrinal preaching might not be considered of the
first order, yet his application of truth, his pathetic appeals to the
heart and conscience of his hearers, and his abundant labours could but,
and almost invariably did, arouse the unthinking and lukewarm to a correct
and proper conception of religious truth and their relations to God and
eternity; that would lead to action, to faith, repentance and obedience;

72

so that after laying the foundation of a correct solid religious experience, and practice, the promises and threatenings of the Gospel were presented and enforced, and as a result as already stated elsewhere, a gracious revival of religion grew up and many that sat in the region and shadow of death, embraced the light and were converted to God.

He rode a large fleet, roan horse, a fine traveler, and when he became delayed in getting on in time to his appointment he put old Roan through. And this was no uncommon thing for him to get behind time, in pursuing his regular habit, to call and pray at nearly every house he passed, saint and sinner. Hence his congregations would often follow him in crowds to his appointments. His motto was never disappoint a congregation;whatever obstructions would at times intervene, his plan was to overcome them. One incident will be sufficient as an illustration. During the summer of that year, while he had his young men with him,he held a meeting of several days on Red Creek at the house of Bro. Thomas Evans during which and several days after, it rained incessantly so that the streams which he had to cross after leaving there were very full; bottoms and swamps completely submerged, and after preaching at my father's neighborhood and at the Red Creek church on the River Road, he found great difficulty in getting over Red Creek, but finally with his young men they succeeded; came on to Black Creek, which was then near a mile wide, and the ferry boat on the opposite side. Here he found two or three other men (citizens) water bound also. Now what to do, was the next thought. All said no chance to get over. Well, says Applewhite, I have an appointment to night at Bro. Bilbo's and must get to it; now one of you will go with me, we will swim over and get the boat. Not one of them, preachers or citizens, would venture. Well, said he, when duty calls I must go and God, I believe, will protect me. And in he went, swimming a while, and taking hold of the bushes awhile to rest a little, and when he came to the main current, he swam across to the other side, and then continued as before, until he finally reached the boat, brought it back, and they all landed safely on the opposite side; got to his appointment that night and God blessed him and his congregation.

I was then teaching school near Judge Fairleys on the road leading to his next appointment, and well do I remember, this religious squad of preachers padding next morning under whip and spur for their next appointment, who by their desire and my solicitation, left an appointment at my school house to be filled on their next round. The time rolled on, the preachers were on hand, the school house crowded with Presbyterians, Methodists and sinners. Bro. Carney preached a good sermon; Bro. Applewhite exhorted and as his usual custom was, invited penitents forward for prayers, had an interesting meeting for that place; for that place, mixed up as it was the congregation of different orders. Some of the old Scotch Presbyterians I don't think fully accorded with the preacher calling for penitents, otherwise spoke favorably of the meeting and preaching.

There were two camp meetings that year on that circuit. One at Dantzlers camp ground on Leaf River and one in my Father's neighborhood, a new camp ground, at both of which good was accomplished. At the first named, Bro. John Bilbo of the Mississippi conference from west of the Mississippi had just returned with his wife on a visit to his Father and Mother; who preached with considerable power and acceptability, having made improvements in many respects. He also attended the one in Father's neighborhood. Brother Anthony S. Dickinson from the Chickasawha Circuit was also at the Dantzler camp meeting. This was the first year of his itinerant life. He still survives as one among the few of the original members of the Alabama Conference.

One other incident connected with this year, makes it to me a memorable one. I had been a church member from the 26th of September 1826, but from timidity and as I thought incompetency and correctly too, had done nothing for God, in the way of work, further than attention to public worship, a moral, upright life, and feeling all the time I ought to do more, and be more efficient in the cause of Christ. But invariably these impressions would be banished by the recollection of incompetency, want of education and so on, backed by an exceeding timidity and fear of the scoffs of others, together with the apprehension of failure and the probability that God did not require it. In this condition, I did not enjoy what I conceived to be my duty and privilege "a growth of grace". And was often led to doubt whether I ever was converted; and consequently was in what we call a backslidden condition. Not conscious of being guilty of any crime for which I ought to be cut off from the church; but by neglect of duty and for the want of an aggressive spirit, became cold, dead and indifferent so that I had no real spiritual enjoyment. I became alarmed at my situation and felt that it would not do to remain as I was. And at several

74

Editor's Notes:

Page 65 - John R. Longino's marriage to Ann Ramsey. <u>Four Centuries on</u>
<u>the Pascagoula</u> by Cain refers to him as John Thomas Longino, Jr. son
of John Thomas Longino, Sr. and Mary Ransom. Since this manuscript is
a WPA typescript, it is possible that the middle initial should be T
instead of R.

School in Copiah County - Isaac Ryan, Soloman Dearman and John McCraney
had previously lived in Jackson County. Here is evidence of the migration
of residents of Jackson County to the Hinds County area.

John B. Short is not shown on the Jackson County, MS census for 1820.
Apparently he came into Jackson County after 1820, moved to Lawrence
County, and was back in Jackson County, MS by 1830 where he is
enumerated on the 1830 Census.

Page 66
Mr. Kirby is unidentified. There are no Kirbys listed in either the
1820 or 1830 census of Mississippi.

Mr. Brooks is unidentified.

See <u>History of Methodism in Alabama</u> and <u>History of Methodism in Mississippi</u>
for biographical sketches of clergymen.

Page 67
Bro. Holder is Willis Holder

Lewis Parker is listed in 1820 Census of Jackson County, MS

See previous notes on John McRae.

Page 68
Brother Andrew's marriage to Nancy Holder. She was the daughter of Willis
Holder. Andrew Ramsey's second marriage to Caroline Evans who was the
daughter of Thomas Evans.

According to <u>Mississippi Harvest</u> by Nollie Hickman "A. W. Ramsey,who
represented Harrison, Perry and Greene and Jackson Counties in the state
Senate in 1850, was adjudged by his colleagues to be the best dressed man
in that body. Every stitch of his clothes except a silk shirt was made
by his wife on a hand loom".

Andrew Ramsey is buried in Leaf Cemetery in Greene County, near the site
of the school that he wanted his children to attend. His marker reads
"Hon. Andrew W. Ramsey, 1-14-1806/4-2-1861, and bears a Masonic emblem.

Page 69
Wyatt Dupree was the son of Sterling Dupree and his wife Abigail Parker.
Sterling Dupree was active in the West Florida Rebellion and was a
colorful character. Legend has it that Sterling Dupree was a friend of
the notorious pirate Lafitte and that Dupree was a whickey runner. More
about the Dupree family before they came to Mississippi Territory can be
found in <u>The Chronicles of Pitt County, North Carolina</u>.

Thomas Bilbo and his brother, William R. Bilbo, can both be found on the
1820 census of Jackson County, MS

Editor's Notes:

Page 70
Joseph & William sons of Thomas Bilbo.

Page 71
Allen McLendon, Esq. - I did not find Allen McLendon listed on the
Jackson County, MS census but did find an Alex McLendon. It is
possible that the census transcription is in error.

Judge John Fairley lived near present day Benndale in George County, MS.

Constable Tucker - Thomas J. Tucker of Jackson County 1830 Census.
Mr. Devise - unidentified
Page 72
Squire McLendon, Bilbo & Dupree - see previous notes.

Col. Morris - probably J. J. H. Morris of Perry County.

Col. Sterling - unidentified

Col. Alsberry - probably Hanson Alsberry of Perry County.
Col. Damevon is probably Dameron. Unidentified.
Page 73
Bro. Thomas Evans - father in law of Andrew Ramsey

Bilbo - Thomas Bilbo

Judge Fairleys - near Benndale in present day George County, MS.

Page 74
Dantzler's camp ground on Leaf River - In Greene County, MS. John L.
Dantzler.

of Bro. Applewhite's meetings I went forward as a penitent and backslider,
but found no alteration in my religious experience and feelings, until
I gave myself up to God; willing to consecrate myself to him and his
work, and if it was His design to assign me any particular work in his
vineyard I would by His grace and assisting, try to perform it. I then
found peace, felt that "God had restored to me the joy of his salvation"
and had not taken His Holy Spirit from me.

So at the camp meeting at Fathers, I made these pledges, privately,
at first between me and my God. Had never said a word on the subject to
any one, nor they to me; until Monday morning, when the meeting closed,
and I was about to leave to resume my labours in my school. In bidding
Father and Mother good bye, Mother asked me what I intended to do after
my school was out. Would I get another school and continue to teach & c?
I was filled with emotion, but made out to communicate my feelings to
her. I remarked, I think not, Mother. I feel it is my duty to try to
preach and by the help of God I feel like trying to do so. She at once
burst into a shout, exclaiming her prayer was answered and right there
and then she and father gave me up in the spirit of sacrifice to God,
promising me their prayers would follow me wherever God saw proper to cast
my lot. And I know as long as they lived, their prayers were offered up
to God for me. My school did not close until about the first of February
following. During Christmas holidays I went home. At night Father said
to me "my son hold family prayers to night". And O what a cross, but I
took it up, did the best I could and I think that first public prayer was
probably as an humble one as I ever offered up since. Christmas that
year came on Sunday and old brother Shoemaker had an appointment on that
day at Bro. Evans which I attended and nothing would do, but for me to
hold service at night. A great cross as I never had appeared before a
congregation in that capacity, but as I had decided and promised God, to
work for him, probably as well commence here as anywhere, among my old
friends and pupils; so I agreed; went into the woods with my Bible; read
and prayed earnestly for divine aid; went back to the house, and lo and
behold! there was the devil right before me or one of his servants, as I
thought, sent there to scare me out of what little I might be able to say.
Mr. John McDonald, a member of the Legislature, on his return from Jackson
had stopped to spend the night. The Devil got after me, and told me I was

*I concluded the service by
singing and prayer which was
the first prayer I had ever
offered in a public congregation.

for consenting to try and hold forth. But I mustered up fortitude and
concluded this man was nothing but a poor sinner; and if it was my duty to
warn such at all, I had as well commence with this big one, as any other.
I read, after singing and prayer, the fourth chapter of Hebrews and from
it made such comments and remarks as presented themselves to my young and
undisciplined mind. This was the first time I had ever stood before a
congregation and the beginning of my ministerial life. And now as I look
back to that night over the forty nine years that will soon elapse, I thank
God that I there started, and that God's grace has sustained me thus far.
- - During this year brother Andrew and wife embraced religion and united
with the Church. He was afterwards appointed one of the stewards of the
circuit and was an efficient one. — 1832 —

The conference which convened in the latter part of 1831, appointed
to the Leaf River Circuit, for this year, Samuel Graves and Enoch N.
Talley who were on hand in due time and served the church faithfully that
year sowing fresh seed of divine truth and gathering fruit from that which
had been sown by their worthy predecessor. My school at Judge Fairley's
had not closed at the time of the first round of appointments on the
circuit. One of which was at Bro. Bilbos at night; about four or five
miles below I met the senior preacher, Bro. Graves, at that appointment;
who had passed and seen father and mother from whom he had learned my
intention and purposes. He at once laid hands on me and insisted on my
getting ready by his next round, as my school would close by that time, and
go with him on the circuit, promising to give me every assistance in his
power, to which I reluctantly consented. This reluctant assent was superinduced, first from a fear that probably I was about to engage in a work
to which God had not designed or called upon me to perform. And which
fear I retained for years after. Another was the fact of a want of that
intellectual culture and an acquisition of thorough religious thought and
a knowledge of Theology that I then believed, and do now, so very important
and indispensible to a successful ministry. Besides all these reasons,
there was another which I feared would prove to be an insuperable barrier
to a continuance were I to make a start, my general health was such and
had been through life that the labour, exposure and exercise of the lungs
incident upon such an undertaking would very soon as I feared force me
to desist and abandon the work. Having had that most distressing disease
Asthma through life, I felt that the undertaking would be a hazardous one.

78

And probably I should, to use a common phrase, break down and make a failure.

Being honest and sincere in my convictions of duty, first to know what duty was and then ability to discharge that duty, formed the difficulties in my mind to a hearty, responsive and willing assent to the proposition of the good brother who met me at every point in a mild christian spirit and arguments, endeavoring to banish from my mind all such fears by referring me to many appropriate passages of scripture such as "My grace is sufficient". "I can through Christ strengthening me, do all things." (Paul) and as I had already commenced, he quoted "He that putteth his hand to the plow and looketh back is not worthy of the Kingdom" &c.; and closed his arguments by remarking, "Make the trial and if you find from an honest effort your health will not sustain and justify your continuance in constant active work, you can but stop and occupy such a sphere or position in the church as will be adapted to your strength." Thus I was led to promise him I would try to be ready to go with him on his next round. And accordingly made the necessary arrangements and met him at the first quarterly meeting at Dantzlers, where the presiding elder Rev. Ebenezer Hearn attended, and where I received from Bro. Graves written by the Presiding Elder, my first official authority to exercise my gifts and graces in the Methodist Episcopal Church as an Exhorter. This was early in 1832. From this point, we started. Bro. Graves first appointment was at Augusta where we were hospitably entertained at the house of Bro. and Sister Dameron. Bro. Graves preached in the Court House, to a very small and I think careless congregation. His pulpit was the Judges stand; a very high one; perched up on the wall some distance. He took me up with him to conclude the service; the first time I had ever occupied such a high position, on such occasions, and which to me was not only an awkward but quite an embarrasing one, so much so, I trembled, turned pale, could scarcely read a very familiar hymn which I had selected; the intonations of my voice altogether changed, so that I know some in the congregation said to themselves at least "that young fellow is scared". And indeed, he knew this himself. The attempt at prayer was no better. In fact I did not know what I said and how it was said. I then intended to retrace my steps and go home and so informed Bro. Graves. He asked me why, I told him if the good Lord designed me for such work, He certainly would arm me with fortitude enough to stand before such a congregation, as we had today, made up of a few nice white folks and some free negroes

without being nearly scared to death. Hence I believed I was in the wrong
place. "O,"said he, "that will never do, that court house, that congregation, that lofty pulpit and a prayerless mixed up little crowd of whites
and mulattoes is enough to embarras any one▽ "I confess,"said he,"it was
a task for me to try and preach to them. Wait, let's go on and get out
into the country where there is more religion than here and you will get
along better; my next appointment is up here about eight or ten miles
tonight on Boguchoma, at old brother and sister Blackledges Church; and
you must preach there tonight; it will be dark, for I know they will not
have the church well lighted; and if you do feel a little scared the
people will not be able to see it as they did, as you think, today in the
court house." So at dinner that day he told Sister Dameron of my
difficulties and what I had proposed whereupon the good sister encouraged
me, and remonstrated with me to give up all such notions; that such were
the embarrasments of all young preachers who were sincere, and relying
upon God for help said "I would rather see you thus embarrased and trembling than to see you, like some I have seen, get up in a pompus, self-
important air, as though they were the only ones who knew anything in the
world". "Such", she said, "got their growth too soon, never advanced much
beyond their first size." Go on she said, read,study, pray much and you will
under God's blessing succeed. This good sisters exhortation started me
out afresh, determined by God's grace to profit by it; and I trust I did.

   Note:- This timidity has followed me through all my ministerial life,
have never gotten fully over it. And often, no doubt, has been detriment-
al to my usefulness. In the first years of my ministry, old and experienced
preachers in the congregation, have often embarrased me to such an extent
that my efforts to me, at least, were failures.

   At other times, it probably was a benefit to cause me to look with
stronger confidence to Him who alone could impart strength and help.
Whether this was the result of man fearing or pleasing spirit, prompted
by pride or vain glory or the great burden and conscious responsibility
of the position coupled with a sense of inadequacy to discharge these
weighty responsibilities, I cannot fully determine. But in the main I
am disposed to think, where it exists in a sincere honest heart,desiring
conscientiously to do the will of God, it arises from the latter and not
the former cause. And this I trust was and has been the principal cause
in my case.

But to return after introducing this note. We left Augusta, and that evening found us in the neighborhood of Blackledges church; night approached; my heart beating faster than usual; tried to beg off, but no! "you must go forward tonight". What to do I hardly knew, went to the woods, tried to pray, but thought or felt like my prayers did not rise higher than my head. Must I take a text? I asked. "Yes, of course, if you wish to do so", was my serious reply. Time arrived, we met a good country congregation, and sure enough the house was badly lighted, one or two candles furnished the light and that but dimly. Service commenced; singing and prayer; and then a portion of scripture read from which a text was selected; and if my memory serves now to be correct; it was in the first chapter of Isaiah. "If ye be willing and obedient ye shall eat the good of the land" & c The scare had nearly passed off and I got along better than I had expected. Bro. Graves brought up the rear, and we had quite an interesting service.

From this point we proceeded onward, around that large circuit, filling appointments at Eucutta, Linders, Simpsons, and many others. Some in Perry, Wayne, Covington, and Hancock as low down as Pearlington. Nothing very remarkable transpiring except having good meetings and the scare wearing off of me gradually until we got to Pearlington, where I had another big one in concluding the service for Bro. Graves. This discouraged me very much so that I resolved to stop when we got around to Fathers. But when I got home, Father and Mother objected to my course and said to Brother G. if you have any use for him, take him on with you. And to me they said it won't do for you to give up so soon; hold on, every one has to have a beginning; have to learn and acquire a knowledge of any business before they can prosecute that business with success. "Go on, go on, my son, you will overcome all these embarrasments by perseverance and reliance upon God". So here I found no sympathy in favor of a relinquishment of the work which I had undertaken. So here I decided to try another round. And very soon after we left Fathers, Bro. Graves told me when we got down on the river, to Red Creek Church at or near Capt. Snells, he would leave me as he wished to visit his father at Mobile and I must go on and fill the appointments alone as far as Eucutta where he would meed me. Said I, "Bro. Graves that will never do, I cannot think of such a thing", but he remonstrated with me until I finally gave in and consented to try. Hence I became what was then called a "Circuit Rider" for one week or more at least. And I have often looked back to that weeks work as being the means

in God's providence of confirming my faith, that my labours would not be
in vain in the Lord; and that I was in the path of duty. My first
appointment was at Bro. Bilbos in the evening where I met many friends,
school mates and pupils that I had taught. I talked to them the best I
could, called for mourners, several came forward, some of the older
members shouted in praise of God and I felt God was with us in mercy and
love. This encouraged me. Took courage and went forward. My next appointment was at Ezekiel Cowarts the next day at 11 o'clock and at McLendon's
church in the evening, both of which I met promptly at the time appointed.
The congregation at Brother Cowarts was made up mostly of his family and
relatives, all Methodists and religious people, quite excitable, when happy
would shout and praise God aloud. In the congregation that day there
were two men, my old acquaintenances and friends, who did not belong to
our church. Malcolm Taylor and Alexander Fairley, the latter my old school
teacher, who taught me in 1820 when I was a little boy. To try to preach
or talk on religious subjects before these men was indeed a heavy cross.
But having committed myself to God and relying upon His grace to strengthen
me for the battle, I went forward in His fear; opened the services; took
my text from Proverbs "The Righteous is more excellent than his neighbor"
God blessed me in the effort; the Methodist appeared happy; many shouts
and praises went up from that congregation. At the conclusion of which I
announced I would supplement the service by a class meeting. Thinking that
what I lacked in one thing, I would try and make up in another. The
congregation being small, I requested all to stay in and so they did.
Taylor and Fairley both remained. And knowing they both had been brought
up in, and I supposed still adhered to, the Presbyterian Church, I felt it
a considerable cross to examine them in Methodist style. But I overcame
this cross before I got to them; as quite an excitement took place with
the others as I passed round examining each one separately and finally I
approached Mr. Taylor and asked him some few questions. he remarked,
"Young man I'm a sinner. I see my sins, but don't feel them as I know I
ought to; you know I was brought up in the Presbyterian Church, a strictly
moral man; but as to this religion that these people profess to feel that
makes them shout, and appear to be so happy under it, I know nothing about
it. And if that is real and genuine, I want it; want to feel it; and hope
if it be real I may yet experience it." I gave him such advice as I thought
applicable to his case; knowing from his character and the sincere develop-

ment of his feelings as brought out by him in this talk, that he was truly
honest and had given me an earnest statement of his real condition; and
after talking to my old school teacher I closed with prayer especially
for my old friend Taylor, presenting to God his case as a sinner who saw
his sins but could not feel then & c. When we arose the good old man was
in tears and in bidding me farewell thanked me for the interest I had
manifested for him. His wife, although not present, was a member of our
church; a good pious woman; whom, in speaking of her, he (Taylor) always
called her "Peggie" an abbreviation of Margaret. He went home that day
feeling worse than he ever had before; divulged his feelings to Peggy;
told all what had transpired that day; the interest the young man had taken
in him & c. Of course she felt concerned for and interested in his spiritual welfare and gave him such counsel as she thought appropriate. His
feelings grew worse and worse; betook himself to private prayer and medi-
tation. This feeling was on Friday, the next day (Saturday) he had to
go into the range to gather up some of his cattle; probably in search of
one to slaughter for a beef; still feeling badly; reflecting on the condition of his soul, began now not only to see that he was a sinner, but to
feel it earnestly. At length, when several miles from home, entirely
alone in the woods, he resolved to stop there and pray. Accordingly he
alighted from his horse hitched him and humbled himself at the trunk of
a large pine tree; and there agonized with God; pouring out before him
bitter cries and tears; promising his God if he would only remove the
burden from his heart and give him peace, so as to satisfy his mind that
"religion of the heart and not so much of the head is that which is taught
and recommended in the Bible as the one thing needful; and only surety
against the vengance threatened to ungodly men, he would give himself
and consecrate his life to His service. Whereupon God spoke peace to
his troubled mind; joy sprang up in his soul and the first thing he knew
he was on his feet, like the lame man in the Acts of the Apostles "walking
and leaping and praising God". Making the words resound with shouts and
halleujahs to God. The great mystery of experimental religion was then
and there, while alone where no eye but the eye of God beheld him, completely solved. He turned his course, retraced his steps and went home to tell
Peggy and his neighboring friends "what great things the Lord had done
for him" which was to her and them, good news and great joy. No longer did
he doubt a religion that inspired the spirit of shouting and praise. These

83

facts I had from his own mouth afterwards; and from several of his
neighbors to whom he had communicated them; and in telling it over to
them again and again would frequently remark that he believed God sent
that young man there that day to be the means in saving his poor soul,
and thanked God that he held that class meeting that day.

The next round on this circuit, Brother Graves and Brother Applewhite exchanged. Bro. Applewhite travelled to the White Sand Circuit
in the bounds of which Bro. Graves lived. Bro. Applewhite wishing to
see his old friends on the Leaf River where he had travelled the year
before and being somewhat an accomodation to Bro. Graves to be with his
family more, the exchange was made. Now I had a new leader and counsellor
this round and be it remembered he pushed me to keep up with him. He,
as formerly stopping and praying at almost every house, Old Roan fat and
sleek knew almost every path and stopping place of the year before, ready
when started for a long sweeping pace, I behind him mounted also on a
fine Roan with a long swinging trot, often pressed to keep up, but invariably coming up to the next stopping place in time; Learned a little
more that round than I had before of some of the felicities of the Itinerant
life. I must here, while referring to horses, notice one fact connected
with the training of Bro. Applewhite's horse Roan. I have called him
old Roan, yet he was not old, about in his prime; he invariably, when he
arrived at the church, would take off his saddle and turn him loose to
graze and cool. Roan would feed around until he heard the noise of
preaching, singing or shouting cease at the church, and frequently had he
been known to come up at full speed to the church house and sometimes,
if the congregation had not left the house, go to the door and look in;
as much as to say "I am ready, Master, come lets go." At others, if he
happened not to be so prompt his master had only to call out, "Come Roan"
and he was soon there in the custody of his Master. He never attempted to
leave or stray off, was certainly the best itinerant horse I ever saw.
The brethern at Cowarts during this interval had finished their log church
house; which was under way when I was round there before; a very comfortable
house of the kind; conveniently located to the whole community. When Bro.
Applewhite and I arrived in sight we saw several of the congregation out
side, apparently looking out for us among whom was my friend Taylor. We
had heard before we got there of his conversion and some of the particulars.
He met me while I was hitching my horse with open arms; praying God's blessi:

upon me, apparently, and no doubt was delighted to see me, as I was to meet
him, not now as a sinner as before, but as one "clothed and in his right
mind". Gave me and Bro. A full account of the dealings of God with him and
his happy conversion & c.

Brother Applewhite preached, called for mourners. Taylor walked
deliberately to his two daughters in the congregation, led them to the
mourners seats and then came to me and said "I want you to pray for my
daughters and hope your prayer may have as good effect on them as it did
on me. After several prayers the door of the church was opened. Mr.
Taylor followed by his two daughters joined. He lived a consistent pious
member of the church for several years after, when under that destructive
disease, consumption, he died and I was informed kept the faith, and left
behind him good hope of his final salvation.

This man's conversion, attended and superinduced by the weak instruments
and agencies, outwardly brought in contact with his mind and conscience
and under God producing such effects and fruits, completely established
me in my purposes for the future. I no longer repined and desired to stop
and abandon the field or to cease using the weapons, although small and
weak, with which the good Lord had endowed me in carrying on the warfare
against the Adversary, but by the help of God felt more determined than
ever to push the battle into the enemies lairs until the citadel and fort-
resses of sin should be besieged and demolished if possible. Feeling more
certainly than ever "that the weapons of our warfare were not carnal, but
mighty through God to the pulling down of strong holds". That if I could
not man the large field pieces, be an artilarist in the battle, I probably
could of execution in the cavalry or infantry ranks by using smaller arms.
The thought crossed my mind time and again that if God had used me, a
mere boy, deficient in many ways as I was, and had blessed the effort to
the awaking of this one sinner who greatly my senior in age, an intellectual culture possibly ought I any longer to doubt that our sufficiency was
of God; and "the battle did not belong to the strong or the race to the
swift". And that God often used "the weak things of the world to confound
the wise". Hence I took fresh courage, and went forth, often sowing in
tears and enduring hardships and afflictions, mentally and physically;
and thank God to day that I have never willfully or wantonly abandoned
the field. Have been engaged in many severe battles and whether or not
I have ever under God achieved any or many victories, Eternity will
disclose.

85

But to return to my narrative. I followed Bro. Applewhite around,
had many precious seasons; some conversions and accessions. And when this
round was performed I again joined Bro. Graves at my fathers where he
brought my case before the church there of which I was a member for a
recommendation for license to preach which was granted me; and at the
next quarterly meeting which met at Dupriests church in Perry County,
I was authorized officially to use my gifts and graces as a Local
Preacher. Thus I continued to labour with Bro. Graves on this circuit
until fall of the year, when I attended a camp meeting at Salem Camp
Ground where I was converted and joined the church in 1826. Here I
tried to preach once or twice and as I thought with some considerable
liberty. Bros. F. A. Jones and Newt Drew were the preachers that year
on that, the Chickasawha Circuit, who had another appointed Camp Meeting
in Greene County at old Bethel Church in old Father McRae's neighborhood,
and the church at which father and mother at an early day held their
membership to which allusion has been made in the former part of this sketch.
The only preachers at this camp meeting were the two circuit preachers,
myself and Uncle "Leven" McRae, a colored man and slave of Father McRae.
And as I have not noticed this colored brother in my sketch, must be per-
mitted to say a few things of him and for him here. As I regard the
Apostles maxim and instructions to be just, to render to all their dues,
among which is "Honor to whom Honour is due". Uncle Leven was, and his
name yet, is entitled to this mark of respect. As already stated he was
a slave, but enjoyed the blessing of a good Christian master, allowing
him many privileges, instructing him in the elementary branches of an
education and allowing him the privileges of leaving from his own family
or others so that his acquirements in this line enabled him to read
fluently. And being endowed with an investigating intellect and by strict
application to reading the Bible and other books at his command, and
above all having the grace of God in his heart, a bright satisfactory
Christian experience, sustained by an upright deportment among whites
and coloured, he became a good, sound, practical and doctrinal preacher,
loved and admired by all who knew him. Had the privilege of going far and
near to preach to his people where often he would have good congregations,
unfolding and enforcing the Word of Life. I presume there were no
preachers in all that Chickasawha and Pascagoula Country, white or black,
that done as much good among the col^d people as Uncle Leven.

86

At the camp meeting above mentioned, Uncle Leven preached or exhorted several times, much to the edification of his white hearers. His old master Father McRae was now dead, and he was still at the old homestead, which had fallen into the hands of the old gentleman's son Dr. David McRae. Whatever became of Uncle Leven, I have no means of knowing, but if his privileges were afterwards as before the death of his old master, I have no doubt(as I suppose he is dead) that he died in the faith and is safe.

After this camp meeting I returned home, met Bro. Graves, who had now procured from my church a recommendation to the fourth quarterly conference as a suitable person to join the travelling connection. The quarterly meeting came on at Dantzler's Church; presided over by Ebenezer Hearn. Brother Graves also brought up from the western part of the circuit from a society on Pearl River, a recommendation, of like import from Bro. Theophilus Moody. And after passing the ordinary examinations, we were both recommended to the Alabama annual conference which was to meet at Tuscaloosa. From this we both returned home, to make suitable arrangements for attending this annual conference.

During this interval my Uncle George Huey who lived in Bibb County, Alabama visited us to see his Father and Mother and sisters who were then alive and lived on our place. I made my arrangements to go back with him and spend a few days there and then go on to Tuscaloosa. Which I accordingly did. But had like to have lost my horse in swimming him across the Cahawba River by the side of a canoe which was a very awkward and clumsy one and pitched into a thick clump of bushes and trees. I holding the bridle kept his head above water while he managed to untangle his limbs and we pushed forward so that he struck bottom and got out safely, much to the joy of my heart. This was on Sunday morning; I had an appointment and tried to preach that day in a little, shabby church and to a little congregation of apparent careless listeners. Spent that night and next day with Uncle John Huey and on Tuesday morning started for Tuscaloosa, which place I reached Wednesday morning. Rode up in front of the Hotel where a gentleman met me, asked my name and remarked "I suppose you have come to attend the conference". I told him I had. Said he "light, my name is Walker. It proved to be Rev. R. L. Walker, the stationed preacher in the Methodist church of that place and to whom was assigned the duty of providing homes for the preachers. I was soon assigned to my quarters,

87

and my horse taken charge of and cared for; and for that week I had nothing
to do but attend the sittings of the conference, witness and learn the
working of this machinery of the church, attend public worship, form new
acquaintances & c and upon the whole had an exceeding pleasant time.

The last night of the conference, the appointments were to be read
out; but before this the Sacrament of the Lords Supper was administered
by Bishop Andrews who presided at the conference and I believe about his
first after his election to that office. During this communion, I was
sitting by Brother Job Foster who was quite an excitable man; would rip
and charge about, exhort and cut many antics when he was happy as he
called it. All at once he became spasmodically excited, laid hold on
me and such was his grip on me that it appeared he would squeeze me to
death and it was with difficulty that I tore myself loose from his grasp.
I thought and would like to have told him, if you are happy, your religion
makes others miserable and of a style that I at least did not covet.
All at once he rose to his feet, run up the aisle of the church, cavorting
and talking, enjoying it all alone, for there were none others who enjoyed
the occasion in that kind of style; but many condemned it. It was said
that some of the young men at the back part of the church remarked after
he got over his excitement or probably while he was up there among them,
"We shall have to put side lines on that fellow to hold him in his place
or he will kill himself or some one else."

Little did I think then that I was to be his colleague for the
next year; but so it turned out. When the Bishop read out the appointments
it was in one case Chickasawha Circuit, Job Foster and A. C. Ramsey.

The next morning off for Chickasawha Circuit, the senior and junior,
which was reached in due time; first appointment was at Providence,
Bro. William Godfrey's church in Washington county, Alabama. Bro. Foster
preached and as it was a four weeks circuit, each one of us had to travel
two weeks apart, one after the other, and thus we travelled the entire
year. I accompanied my colleague from this first appointment several days
with him at several appointments and then returned, and commenced my round
at the starting point Providence. Here I met a good congregation to which
I tried under great embarrassment to deliver my message, but through much
fear and trembling so much so that a good sister, with whom we had lodged
when there before at Bro. Fosters appointment, asked me if I had not been
sick. I told her no. "Why", said she,"you looked so pale when you arose
in the pulpit today I thought you certainly had been sick". Ah, said I,

88

"sister that was caused by my exceeding embarrassment having to try to preach
before such an intelligent congregation; almost drove from my mind every
thought I had tried to collect"and remarked that there were certain persons
in the congregation that I couldn't bear the idea of trying to teach, viz:
Brother Myers, an old local preacher, Bro. Godfrey and Mrs. John McRae with
whom I had once boarded, while at school on the coast. I feared I should
not be able to conquer this distressing and discouraging besetment at that
place during the year. They encouraged me and expressed sympathy for me.
And here let me notice one fact connected with this despondent and harassing dread of others, as showing that it is generally more the suggestions
of Satan than anything else, leading us to regard certain men as critics,
fault finders, and such like, rather than friends and sympathizers which
could we look into their heart and minds, we would readily see the reverse
of what we had imagined. To illustrate, This Bro. Godfrey that I dreaded
so much, and at whose house I had stopped on my way to Tuscaloosa, and of
whom I had always heard a very favorable report, a pious, exemplary Christian gentleman, and which from further acquaintance I found to be altogether
correct, was to me such a cross that I broke down when asked to say grace
at his table; and also in conducting family worship at night and also the
night before my first appointment above alluded to, I stopped with him
again; a wedding was on hand, one of his step daughters was married and
such was the dread and embarrassed feelings anticipated at the table, that
I actually refused supper. Bro. Myers conducted family worship. Next
morning, it was equally as bad at the table and family prayer. I made
out however, in a trembling, stammering way to get through the dreaded task.
After this I determined when in that neighborhood not to go again to Brother
Godfreys. Nor did I for several rounds although invariably solicited to
do so, by this good and noble brother. He, at length, after insisting
on me at the church at one of my appointments, to go with him and I refusing,
said "Bro. Ramsey, what is the matter? Why is it you will not go to my
house? Is there anything wrong?" "Well,"said I, "my brother I will tell
you nothing wrong on your part, but there is on mine. You are such a cross
to me, that I cannot ever ask a blessing at your table, hold family prayers,
or preach before you, without being choked up and embarrassed to such an
extent that I lose almost every thought I have and have no liberty of speech
while in your presence, so that I decided not to go back until this dreadful
besetment would wear off". Which I had no doubt you have discovered when I

stopped with you in the early part of the year. At other places it is not
so. "Why God bless you my young brother, you have not a better friend in
all this country than I am; one who prays for you and your success more
fervently. I know you are young and just commencing the work and, of course,
these embarrassments will attend any young man at first, who is sincere, and
trying to learn and do the work to which he believes God has assigned him."
Now don't let Satan cause you to suppose that your friends are your enemies;
come along and go home with me and I hope these feelings will wear off and
you will yet become a true, faithful and successful preacher for be assured
my brother, these are suggestions of the Devil." This affectionate and
fatherly talk had the designed effect, removed all such feelings from me.
I went home with him and never after this was Brother Godfrey any cross to
me. Spent much time with him on my rest days to whose valuable library
I had free access and from which I derived some valuable assistance. And
with whom and whose nice family I thought I became a favorite.

From this first appointment I proceeded on, meeting all my appointments
and met Bro. Foster at his mother-in-laws (Sister Campbell) about half way
the circuit on the Chickasawha River; and from a judicious arrangement of
the appointments the circuit formed the shape of the figure 8 at center of
which was Sister Campbells where we met every round. Brother Drew from the
Leaf River Circuit had fallen in with us at this point. Brother Foster
communicated to us the fact that he had on this, his first round, formed
or entered into a matrimonial engagement on the lower part of the circuit,
(he being a widower) with Miss Theresa Wells and would marry at his next
round at the first quarterly meeting which was to convene at Salem Camp
Ground a few miles above Father Wells. This was news to us both and not
a little astonishing, that a man and especially a circuit preacher, should
meet a girl whom he had never seen before, fall in love, court her the
first time they met, become engaged, ask for her the next morning, get the
old folks consent, appoint the time for the celebration of the nuptials to
take place at their second meeting, was to us quick work showing that all
hands were easily pleased. And that it did not at all times and with
certain parties require long courtships to cultivate the finer feelings of
affectionate nature each to the other; or that it was not important to
understand fully, the character, standing or temperament of each other in
order to form a suitable alliance; but that going it blind, according to
the old adage, was as good a way as any. And so they thought and so acted.

I performed the balance of the round on the circuit, meeting and
mingling with many old friends and brethren, many of whom I had known from
boyhood and to whom at some few appointments, particularly at my spiritual
birthplace, Salem Camp ground, I had preached a few times the year before.
Here I felt at home among friends and old associates and the communion of
kindred feelings was indeed pleasant, encouraging and profitable to me.
At the house of Father Wells (Bro. Foster's prospective father-in-law) I
met Mr. Stephen F. Pilley who accompanied me the next day to my appointment at Sister Cewmbus; and the same evening to the neighborhood below
where his prospective Mother-in-law, Sister Graham lived. Having conversed
with him on the subject of religion considerably on our way; and stopping
that night at old Uncle Jesse Graves who insisted on having night service
that night at his house, my assent was cordially given; a small congregation
collected and after trying to preach I called for penitents whereupon Mr.
Pilley approached, apparently considerably exercised and knelt down in the
chair before me and behind the back of which I had stood in talking to
them. Several prayers were offered and then and there Br. Pilley professed
to find pardon. The next day at the church he gave me his hand and I believe
God his heart, and became a member of the Methodist E. Church, and subsequently
an able, efficient and exemplary minister of the Gospel and lived and died,
a good and great man, a member of the Alabama conference. Was my colleague
for two years in 1836 on the Leaf River Circuit; in 1837 on the Cedar Creek
Circuit. I published in the New Orleans Advocate the last of 1878 or the
first of 1879, a detailed biographical sketch of this good man and think
it not necessary now to say more of him than I have above or to give here
a repetition of what was in that sketch.

Quarterly meeting now approached, which caused me to lose some few
appointments before I got round on the upper part of the circuit. Met
Bro. Foster on my way up at our meeting point. Insisted on my not going
back to the quarterly meeting and caused me to lose some of my appointments.
But he insisted on my going as a matter of duty & c besides said he "I
want you to be at my wedding to wait on me and see me married". Of course,
I went. Meeting opened on Saturday. Presiding Elder E. Hearn present.
The usual exercises and routine of Quarterly conference business attended
to. No very fine or extraordinary reports of revivals submitted. No
very marked signs as yet of fruit from the little quantity of seed sown,
hopes expressed of a good harvest in the future; a good spiritual feeling
under the word preached and at the communion service.

Editor's Notes:

Page 78 - All persons previously identified in Editor's notes.

Page 79
Dantzler's - John L. Dantzler on Leaf River in Greene County, MS.

Brother and Sister Dameron - C. B. Dameron in Perry County, MS where
Augusta was then the county site.

Free negroes - a family of mulattoes by the name of Clark had settled
in Perry County. A special act of the state legislature was required
for them to live free in Perry County, MS at that time period.

Page 80
Brother and Sister Blackledge on Bogue Homa Creek in Perry County, MS
was Hezekiah Blackledge.

Sister Dameron - see above

Page 81
Eucutta is a community in northwestern Wayne County, MS near the Clarke
County border.

Linder's - John L. Linder in Jones County, MS

Simpson's - either Nathan or Charles Simpson. Both are residing in Jones
County, MS at this time period. They appear to be brothers.

Capt. Snell - Samuel Snell. Bro. Bilbo - Thomas Bilbo

Page 82
Ezekiel Cowart - lived in northern Jackson County (present day George
County) not far from the Greene County border.

McLendon's Church - in the same area as Ezekiel Cowart. McLendon's church
was probably located in the are of the Pipkin Cemetery, George County, MS
This would be section 2 or 3, Township 1 South, Range 8West. Sections in
this area are irregular due to early Spanish land grants.

Malcolm Taylor was a resident of Perry County in 1830. Alexander Fairley
lived in Greene County in 1830. The area where Cowarts and McLendons
lived was not far from either Greene or Perry County - all within a two or
three mile area. Malcolm Taylor's wife was Margaret McRae.

Page 83
Peggie Taylor - see above

Page 84
Cowart's log church - There is today a cemetery in Section 9, Township 1
South, Range 8 West in George County that sits back from the road and
there appears to have been a building in front of it. This was the
location of Ezekiel Cowart's land, and possibly the location of the log
church referred to here.

Page 85
See previous notes on the Taylor family.

Editor's Notes:

Page 86
Father McRae - John McRae

Dupriest's Church in Perry County, MS - James Dupriest and his wife
Penelope Farr and their married children James, Jr., John and William
lived in Perry County in the 1830's. James Dupriest, Jr. had married
first Amelia Atwood and upon her death, Mary Wall widow of Micajah
Wall of Wayne County, MS. John had two wives, names unknown, the second
of which he divorced in Hancock County in 1857; William Dupriest was
married to Sarah Cowart.

Page 87
Dantzler's Church - see previous notes.

Uncle George Huey - brother of A. C. Ramsey's mother. The parents of
George Huey were Andrew and Nancy Huey who had formerly lived in Georgia
and at some time between 1830 and 1832 had come to Jackson County, MS to
live with the William Ramsey family.

Page 88
Bro. William Godfrey's was in Washington County, AL. Providence Methodist
Church still exists today. It is located 3½ miles north of Millry, AL just
off the Millry-Isney road. The oldest marked grave is that of James
Bingham born in Jefferson County, GA 1-1-1805 and died in Washington Counnty,
AL 5-11-1876. There are a number of unmarked graves which may be those
of the early settlers who attended church here.

Page 89
Brother William Godfrey - see above

Mrs. John McRae - was Mary Dubose McRae, widow of John McRae

Brother Myers - unidentified

Page 90
Sister Campbell - widow of Edward Campbell in Wayne County, MS

Miss Theresa Wells, daughter of Father Wells. Father Wells was Henry Wells
who settled on the Pascagoula River in 1811.

Page 91
Father Wells - see above

Stephen F. Pilley - unidentified

Sister Cewnbus - Probably Sister Cumbest. Simon Cumbest had land on the
Pascagoula River in 1799 and John Cumbest on the Escatawpa River in 1810.

Sister Graham - Unsure if this is Laird, Matthew or William Graham. All
three lived in Jackson County, MS in 1830 and all three had daughters of
marriagable age.

93

Sunday's service closed. Presideing Elder, Senior and Junior Preaches now repaired to the house of Father Wells; where a few persons gathered and at the appointed time my venerable Senior and colleague led his betrothe on the floor where the Presiding Elder united them in the bonds of holy wedlock.

The next morning I walked out with Father Wells to look at the quantity of bee hives he had. There were many; and I remarked what are you going to do with so much honey? "Ah,"said he, "they are not mine, they all belong to Theresa. She has better luck with bees than I have had so I gave them all to her." I met Foster and told him he had certainly married more honey than any man in all that country. I think I counted ninety hives. Bro. Foster was very punctual to his work. Lost no appointments by his marrying, done a good faithful years work and was returned to that circuit the next year and travelled the same circuit in 1837 and 38. He was a very impulsive man, eccentric, particularly, as I have elsewhere stated, while under religious excitement. One or two more instances in addition to the one at Tuscaloosa already stated, will demonstrate clearly these qualities. On one occasion the year before this he was on the Tombigby circuit. At a camp meeting at Suggsville he got in one of his ways and was sitting on the straw in the altar talking many ways, happy as he said, but no one ever got happy when he was; all at once he said "I'll bet I die shouting", but bethought himself and said, "If it was lawful to bet." Some of the wicked crowd went off and reported that Foster said "He'd bet his horse he'd die shouting." Except this exaggerated statement, the other was a fact, and told to me by one who was standing by him and heard it. Sister Pritchett as pious and good a woman as was in all that country. Another: At a camp meeting this year, 1833, of the events of which I am writing. We attended in the company with Bro. Paul F. Sterns, from the Mobile Mission, a camp meeting at the camp ground near my mothers. In one of his excitements, in Mother's tent at night, he arose from the ground on which he had been sitting and which was a common thing with him, when thus excited to sit for a while at least flat on the ground, and there talk as to himself, all at once he arose ripping over the tent, kicking over chairs, pushing people here and there and directly approached Brother Sterns who always enjoyed his religion in a quiet calm and composed state of mind; seized him, put his hands on his head, and exclaimed "Brother Saul receive thy sight". These paroxism or spasmodic efforts generally

94

occured at Camp Meetings or large religious gatherings and was the result
of some defect no doubt in his nervous system; something wrong in the
organizm of his nature; subject at times to great despondency, his spirits
would often be so low that he could see no sunshine before him; at other
times high and elevated in his hopes and aspirations. Adversity appeared
to sink him, prosperity to raise him. And looking at him from a religious
standpoint seeing his aversion to evil, in its varied forms, his conformity
to the laws of God, his great and earnest desire for the welfare of his
race, and his devotion to his work. I always regarded and loved Brother
Foster as a good man. Although some may doubt this when I here record
(as I have heard) the end to which he finally brought himself; whether sane
or insane I know not. He moved to Texas and as I have been creditably
informed committed "suicide by hanging himself" Poor Job Foster was not
your mind deranged by an excess of care or trouble?

During this year I was much troubled with Asthma. Dr. Fletcher
who lived on Buckatunna was a steam Doctor, who took me in hand saying
he could cure me, but all the steam, Lobelia, anti spasmodics & c that he
used on me done but little if any good. It still continued and does to
this day. In trying to cross Buckatunna at one time which was swollen and
no flat or ferry boat, but only a skiff in which to cross persons over
was the only water craft kept there; horses had to swam across. I found
the skiff, but the paddle on the opposite side. The skiff which was built
in the form of a flat, but quite small was there nearly full of water, and
I could find nothing by which to bale it out. A rope was stretched across
by which to propell the little craft from one side to the other. Thinking
I could pull the thing over by the rope and get the paddle and bale out
the boat; so I took my stand about the middle of the little concern, could
not stand at either end, for the reason my weight sank it so with the water
inside that it would dip and soon would have been under completely consequently I must balance it by standing in the middle. A negro man was on the
opposite side, about the time I struck the main current the miserable thing
began to turn round, the bow downwards. I saw I could not get it over
in that way and called to the negro to throw me the paddle which he tried
to do, but did not fall near me, some several feet before me. I had now
let go the rope and in stepping to the bow to reach after the paddle down
went the boat. I jumped out, caught the paddle and the boat arose bottom
upwards. I had taken off my coat, hat and shoes and being a good swimmer

got in the rear of the boat and drove it before me. The negro was badly
alarmed and asked if he could help me, said he could not swim. I told him
then not to come in there, but go down about fifty yards where I saw a tree
had fallen in to the creek and meet me there and I would carry the boat to
him which I did; got out, baled the boat and swam my horse over and went
to Dr. Fletchers wet as a drowned rat, but too late to meet my appointment
that day.

On another round, probably my next, I met at Church at Bro. Hendersons
in the Everett neighborhood, Col. John M. Burke of Wilcox County, Alabama,
who was there to get the testimony of a Mr. Finley in an important lawsuit,
in which he was interested in Alabama, and having to go to Winchester, with
this witness, in order to get his deposition and have it legally authenti-
cated; and Mr. Finley having no horse, borrowed mine that evening to ride
round with the Col. and borrow or hire one to ride to Winchester the next
day, and succeeded in doing so. The next morning we were all going the
same road, a part of the way and had to cross this same Bucatunna at the
same place where I had gotten the ducking previously. We soon arrived at
the memorable crossing place where we found the same skiff or little boat,
by which I had been immersed; But lo and behold! it was locked; and the
creek swimming as before. Now said they, "What are we to do?" The little
craft was locked to a small bush or sapling that grew near the waters edge,
in a clump of bushes, the tops of which were covered with vines so that
they were all held together by a complete network. I examined the situation
and knowing that the boat belonged to Mr. Everett, a very clever gentleman,
with whom I was acquainted. I proposed to cut the little sapling to which
the boat was locked and I thought Mr. Everett whom I would inform of what
we had done, would be satisfied provided no loss was sustained. Col. Burke
remarked "if you can get us over and by so doing the owner charges anything
or if there be any damages, write to me and I will pay it, giving his address
So I cut the bush about a foot from the ground, the top perfectly steady
held up by the vines and now had things in ferrying order. Now said the
Col. "how now? how are you going to manage?" Take off your saddles and
baggage from all the horses and put them on the boat, which I soon conveyed
over. Came back, took the two men, deposited them with the baggage and to
catch the horses which I turned in, mine in front and which were soon on
the opposite side, I following them. Now says the Col. again "how are you
going to get the boat back?" I told him I should carry it back as I brought

it over; then how will you get back? I'll swim back. So I dispensed with
my clothing, took the boat back, slipped the chain over the little stump,
put both cut ends together, wrapped it closely with the vine, jumped in and
swam over and soon adjusted clothing and travelling equipage and went on
our way rejoicing; carrying with me the thanks and good wishes of Col.
Burke and his travelling companion; thinking it Providential that he fell
in with the young preacher for said he "but for you, we could not have
gotten over" and thought I was certainly designed for the itinerant work,
especially in that rough and watery country. I met Col. Burk the next year
on the Cedar Creek circuit to which I had been assigned by the conference
and then, and for years after whenever I met him, he invairably related
how his little preacher (as he called him) ferried him over Bucatunna -
the year 1833.

- My Father's Death -

At my appointment in July at Salem Camp Ground, I was met by brother
Andrew, who bore to me the sad news of the death of Father which had
taken place at his home on Red Creek the 19th of that month (July).
This was to me and all the family an afflictive providence. Although he
had been helpless for a number of years, a great sufferer, so that he was
perfectly helpless, not able to feed or dress himself; and to an outsider
looking from worldly side; and relief from care, on our part, and relief
of suffering on his, with the blessed hope of rest hereafter, as entertained
by him. From that stand point, it might have been thought best for both.
But the parental tie had so bound us together and the reverence and affectionate regard which cemented and bound us to him that the labour, anxiety
and care consequent upon nursing and watching over him was not so onerous
as to cause a wish that relief should be obtained only by his death. But
God so ordered it and while we could but weep and lament the sad bereave-
ment we "sorrowed not as those who had no hope". He died at the age of
62 years, 11 months, 22 days. Father was an energetic, economical, manager
in his domestic affairs and these elements coupled with a sound unwavering
faith and Christian exper. in divine things constituted the basis upon which
he built up a moral superstructure of respectability and usefulness where-
ever he lived or among whom he mingled. One worthy the imitation of all.
These virtues and christian graces were not only prominent in health, but
being supplemented by great patience in suffering. It may I think be
justly said, he not only did but likewise suffered the will of God as

97

becometh one of His children. O that his children who yet remain, his long
line of descendants of grand children and great grand children that are
now scattered in Alabama, Mississippi, Texas, Arkansas and Missouri may all
emulate his virtues, die in peace and meet him in Heaven where we humbly
trust and hope he now "rests from his labours and his works follow him, Amen.

The work of that year on the circuit was not marked by extraordinary
manifestations of revival power as a general result, but at some points there
were awakenings and some conversions while the church generally appeared
to be quickened and alive to duty. In the fall our annual camp meeting
took place at Salem. Where the power of God was felt, and its effects seen
in the awakenings and conversions of many souls. But here, as in the days,
of Job "when the sons of God come together the Devil came also". For one
or two nights several fellows of the baser sort had been going round interrupting the tent holders much to the annoyance and discomfort of the ladies
particularly. On Sunday night, it became unsufferable after the congregation
had retired from the stand and many had taken to their beds. A messenger
was sent to the preacher's house (the church) for the preachers to come and
try and put a stop to it. Bro. Foster accompanied by a good large guard
of young men, met the crowd; expostulated with them, advised them, shamed
them, referred them to their parents some of whom were tented on the ground.
This all appeared only as casting pearls before swine; only exasperated
them, so that violence was threatened to him by the ring leader. This,
however, did not intimidate him. He felt himself perfectly able to measure
arms with this son of Beliel. He knew moreover, if an attempt was made on
him, it would be immediately repulsed by the men behind him, some of whom
were anxious to get a chance to frail out this God provoking set. Very
soon an altercation took place between two of them about some little personal
difficulty that arose between two of them that day. The belligerants
were Philip Williams for Foster, Howell for the rowdies. Howel made the
attack, Williams knocked him down and beat him badly until he had to sing
out "enough". Williams' friends stood by and would not suffer any foul
play until Howell's face and eyes were terribly beaten, gouged and bruised,
beside many hard licks under, and on his ribs. Poor fellow he looked
dreadfully used up the next morning. This scattered them; the balance of
the night passed off quietly. The next morning Bro. Foster in closing the
meeting, gave these fellows one of the severest tongue castigations I ever
heard. Told them he did not fear them, he could whip any two of them, and

if they had have jumped on him the night before, he would have shown them; that God would not let such a set as they were abuse him, whip him, &c, &c.

From this meeting Bros. Foster, Sterns and myself repaired to the camp meeting at my Mothers (who was also with us having attended this one at Salem) an account of which I have given in the short sketch of Bro. Foster.

After this meeting closed, I went to Mobile and attended Bro. Sterns' camp meeting at George's camp ground above Mobile in the bounds of what was then called the Mobile Mission. This was a good meeting. The Presiding Elder Ebenezer Hearn, Brother Smith from the Mobile Station and Bro. R. L. Walker of Mobile who had located there and entered into the commission business and also Bro. Newitt Drew from the Leaf River Circuit were in attendance. Large crowds from Mobile and surrounding country attended; mixed up, some good, some not so good especially some of the higher class as they supposed themselves to be; but of the low down scum of creation who came there for sinful purposes. Some of these commenced coming into the altar for prayers, and which was soon seen prevented other decent people from coming. So that Bro. R. L. Walker in a public lecture in the altar, told them in such a way that they took the hint, they were not wanted there, and they stopped coming. In fact he told them they were there at the camp meeting for no good; go home, and bring forth fruits meet for repentance, before they intruded themselves upon decent people. After this no barriers were in the way and quite a number found peace and pardon.

As I am writing from memory, of course I am liable to err, especially in times and dates and may sometimes be compelled in order to notice certain incidents or occasions that preceeded some already mentioned. Which is the case now. I attended camp meeting in the bounds of Bro. Drew's circuit (Leaf River) before I went to Mobile to Bro. Sterns. This slipped my memory at the proper time and place in my narrative.

The camp ground was in the neighborhood of Bro. John Gardners between the Chicasawha and Leaf Rivers. I went from the one at Mothers to this one and afterwards to Mobile. Here were but few preachers. Do not recollect whether Bro. Foster was there or not, but think not. Dr. Fletcher, Bro. Drew, Isham Moody and myself are all I now have any recollection of. We had a real good religious time. Dr. Fletcher I recollect preached very acceptably and good was accomplished, what the precise results I cannot now remember.

99

Editor's Notes:

Page 94
Father Wells – see previous notes.
Theresa Wells Foster – see previous notes.
Suggsville – a community in Clarke County, Alabama

Page 95
Dr. Fletcher who lived on Bucatunna – This would be in Wayne County, MS.
and is probably David Fletcher.

Page 96
Bro. Henderson's church. I believe that this is probably Hendricks
rather than Henderson. The Hendricks family lived in the Bucatunna
area, but there were no Hendersons listed in Wayne County, MS at this
time period.

Mr. Finley – John Finley

Everitt Neighborhood – There were no Everitts listed in Wayne County
at the time. They probably lived just across the state line in the
Isney, Al. area.

Col. Burke – of Wilcox County, AL. Unidentified, but this gives
more evidence that the migrations of families from Greene and Wayne
Counties, MS to the Wilcox County, Alabama area and back again were
prevalent.

Page 98
Philip Williams and Howell – unable to identify. There were several
families of Williams and Howells in Jackson County at this time.

Page 99
Bro. John Gardners between the Chicasawha and Leaf Rivers – Greene
County, MS. Probably John S. Gardner an early settler of Greene
County, however, there were two other John Gardners in Greene County
at that time – John Jr. who married Mattie Walley and John Gardner
who married Martha Roberts.

Dr. Fletcher from the Bucatunna community of Wayne County, MS

Isham Moody and his wife Priscilla Bass lived in Greene County at this
time.

No attempt will be made to identify places or persons on the Alabama
Circuit.

- Rev. Newett Drew -

As I have alluded to this brother, I take the liberty of saying a few
things about him. I went from this camp meeting with him to Bro. John
Dantziers and thence to Mobile together; besides had been with him frequently
during the year and the year before. Hence I think I understood his character. As a preacher, he was ordinary; as an exhorter pathetic and impressive;
hence done good. His education was but limited, yet he improved some in
preaching and culture. Would have advanced more rapidly, could he or would
he have applied himself to study and reading and if he had not been endowed
with an inordinate love of money. Whether natural or acquired, I can not
tell. But which was evidently cultivated to that extent that his mind
was too much absorbed and taken up on that subject to allow much culture
of the better elements of his nature or to make much improvement on subject
of Theology. Hence I think he about had his growth in a knowledge of the
Bible and its truths when I was with him.

As an illustration of this prevailing passion, I will give a few
instances. He saved all his quarterings, turned it all into silver.
Would not even provide himself with neat, nice or comfortable clothing.
Rode an old saddle not fit for a darkey even in those days of slavery.
His bridle was of plow lines. His saddle bags, old, torn and sewed up and
tied with strings. Had a large gray mare, which I presume he started with;
from which he raised while on his circuit the year before a very fine colt,
and which he sold this year for a good price, cash. His old gray brought
him another colt this year; and sold out I believe mare and colt for a
fine price, and made out to get another smaller one very cheap. His gray
was a good animal, of good stock and her colts were fine and salable. He
deposited his money with Miss Irene Dantzler this year. She was the
custodian of his cash. When we were about to leave there for Mobile, she
brought his sack of silver. He had wound up the work on his circuit and
did not expect to return so he wanted to take his money with him. Emptied
the sack on the table and it looked as if there were near or quite a peck
of dollars, half dollars and quarters. I do not know that I ever saw such
a pile of silver before. He rolled, packed and fixed it up in as convenient
bundles as possible, packed it away in his old saddle bags, whihh I really
thought would burst with the weight and spill out before he travelled far,
but in this I was mistaken.

After we started, now said I "Bro. Drew we are going to Mobile and you

have plenty of money, you must go to a clothing store and get you a decent
outfit to wear to conference, besides you need them whether you go to
conference or not. And also go to a saddler's store and get you a decent
bridle, saddle and saddle bags. Do fix up as a preacher ought to". Said
he, "well I'll see about it." But before we got to the city, after giving
him several lectures on the subject, I found he did not intend to do it.
Said he wanted to get him a bridle, if he could get one cheap. Said also
he would like to have a new pair of saddle bags, but didn't know how he
could carry along two pair. Said I "you certainly are not going to carry
off those old ones with you." "O, yes". "Where are you going to take
them to?" "Take them back on Chickasawha and sell them to Dr. Patton
for hog wallets". Dr. Patton lived sixty or seventy miles from Mobile.
This really provoked me. Said I, "Drew you are certainly the greatest
miser I ever saw. You are positively letting down the dignity of the
ministry. Your money will never do you any good, it will perish with you.
Your inordinate love for it will ruin you." "Now", said I, " go with me
when we get there to the stores and I will assist you". "No, I reckon I
can attend to it". "Yes I know you can if you would, but I don't believe
you intend to do it." "How will you feel riding into Mobile in that garb?"
Before we got there, however, he stopped and sorted out some of his paper
money (for he had some of this also) took about seven dollars, I think it
was which he said he would likely spend in the city. Said I, "Is that all
you intend to spend?" "Yes, that will be enough." I could not help exclaiming in my heart "God pity your poor stingy penurious soul"! While we were
entering the suburbs of the city, his pride got the upper hand of him and
his conscience, for one time, checked him. Said "Bro. Ramsey, please loan
me your Buffalo rug to put over my old saddle; it looks so bad going into
town with it." Said I to him, "Bro. Drew, I shall not do it. You may go
as you are and I hope you will still feel worse for a man in your condition
and a preacher of the Gospel, preaching benevolence, decency and order to
others; and too stingy to practice even on yourself what you preach to
others, and prefer to be a slouch rather than give up your grip on those
dollars; may for aught I care suffer the mortification of his pride
and goadings of a guilty conscience as long as time lasts for me; before
I will disrobe myself to accomodate your pride". "Pride and stinginess
are not pleasant bed fellows. If you were an object of charity, I would
do it, but you are not."

We went on and remained in the city until the next day and I could not
get him even to go with me to the stores, but finally when we were getting
ready to leave, he unrolled a little bundle or I believe had it in his
hand, a little thin flanky leather snaffle bridle for which he paid fifty
cents, which was the amount of his purchases. The next year he was assigned
to Baldwin Mission, by Bishop Emory, which lay on the Alabama River below
Claiborne. Here he married a Miss Henderson and the next year located
and settled near Mount Pleasant in Monroe county. Invested his money in
negroes and land and became a farmer; but I think I learned not a very
successful one. In purchasing negroes, as I was told by Bro. Burpo, he
generally bought at public sale without much respect to age or character
because they were cheap. Poor man, he lived there several years and was
finally killed by another man. Thus ended the life of Newitt Drew, who
possessed many good traits of character and, but for this insatiable thirst
for this world's goods, no harm could be said of him and otherwise a good
lovely man.

- Winding up of this year's Work -

Camp meetings being over and one round more to be performed before
leaving for conference, the balance of the year was thus employed, trying
to preach to the people, as I thought possible the last time; bidding them
farewell. A people whom I loved and who had shown me such evidence of
kindness and Christian affection could but produce emotions of sorrow and
sadness that caused many tears to flow from both preacher and people.
Although except in one instance, no farewell sermons or any formal manifestations of leave taking was resorted to; yet we had generally a melting time,
many sobs and sighs were often heard. At Salem, I tried to preach my first
and only valedictory from that old farewell text of the Apostle Paul "Finally
brethern farewell, be perfect & c" while there were many tears shed and much
weeping and regrets expressed at our separation, yet the doubt on my mind
was whether any permanent good was accomplished so I have never repeated
that mode of parting since.

The years work now closed, and I visited my parents and relatives and
left for conference which convened in the city of Montgomery, late in the
season in December, I think. Having made an arrangement with brother Sterns
to join him at Shady Grove neighborhood in Wilcox County, I hastened on
crossing the Bigby at Coffeeville, the Alabama at the Lower Peachtree, I
met Brother Sterns in due time; and after one days rest, we wended our way

up the Alabama River, through the Alabama Circuit, which Bro. S had travelled
the year before, stopping with a brother Jackson with whom I swapped horses
disposing of my long, fast trotting Roan for a sorrel; and which cost me
ten dollars to boot and which the good brother ought not to have required
for my roan was the best horse; except that his hoofs had become diseased
so that it was with difficulty he could travel and was the reason of my
trading him. We spent the Sabbath at Vernon when we joined Bro. Jacob
Matthews, Charles McLeod, and Edward Moore, who had the measles on him then
but did not know it; and from whom I caught them which caused me great
suffering that winter and almost the entire of next year. Bro. J. Matthews
preached on Sabbath.

In due time we were all at Montgomery. Homes assigned us; weather
extremely bad, rain, snow and sleet. My sleeping apartment was in an old
vacated hotel, near the river in company with a crowd of young preachers
and had to go out and get our meals at different places in the city, which
caused so much exposure besides uncomfortable beds and lodging that I was
attacked with a severe spell of Asthma together with the measels now taking
hold of me, so that during the whole session I was a real sufferer, so much
I set out to get another place to lodge and finally after several unsuccess-
ful efforts among the old preachers, Bro. Sterns offered me a berth in his
room. Here there were every comfort of good fires & c. besides the motherly
care of the good sister owning the place; and consequently spent the few
days remaining of the session very comfortably. I shall never forget good
Bro. Paul F. Sterns' kindness.

– The Conference –

Convened at the appointed time. Bishop Emory presided much to the
satisfaction of the brethren. Several visiting brethren present, among
whom was Charles Kennon and Jeremiah Norman of Georgia, both of whom preached
during the session. Business was dispatched by the Bishop, carefully and
safely, so that on Sunday the Ordinations were attended to, the Bishop
preaching at 11 o'clock. And I confess, I had either looked for too much,
set my estimate of the Bishop's preaching abilities too high, or else I was
in a bad condition to hear; probably the last, for I was really disappointed
but in looking round, I saw a number of the older preachers in tears, viz:
Levert R. L. Walker, R. L. Kennon, James Mellard, Ebenezer Hearn, and others
so that I decided certainly the fault was in me, but could not help thinking
that if I was up there saying those identical words, using the same gestures,

103

and intonations of voice, not a tear would have been shed, their heads
would have been hung; perfectly ashamed of me. And I was not the only
one that had such thoughts. Bro. James Thompson from the Cedar Creek
circuit to which I was assigned the next year, an excellent local preacher,
was at that conference for ordination, who heard the Bishop's sermon and
told me he had the same identical thoughts. We both concluded that a position and name had a great deal to do in producing effects by some divines.
Bishop Emory was certainly a good divine; good writer and an intellectual
preacher; but some how or other it did not, to my weak capacity of judging,
so appear that day. In due time the work of the conference was closed and
every one ready to leave, and only waiting for the secret roll to be un-
furled; and receive their appointed sphere of labour for the next year.
The Bishop very gravely approached the stand and announced the

- Appointments -

And on that long list was Cedar Creek Circuit; Isaac N. Mullins
and A. C. Ramsey, who in company with Judge Lane of Greenville were soon
on the road, leading from Montgomery to Greenville. And being a day or
two ahead of time, we stopped at Bro. James McFarlands, who was a steam
Doctor, and commenced on me who had been and was still suffering from
Asthma and Measles, although they had not yet developed, but his remedies
done me no good. Sunday arrived, two appointments to be filled. One at
Spring Hill at 11 A.M. and Greenville at 3 P. M. both of which Bro.
Mullins had to fill. I still continued with him, spent the night at
Judge Lanes but too sick the next morning to go on. Judge Lane advised
to stop and go to Dr. Hillary Herberts and get him to take me in charge,
believing the Doctor would keep me at his house and nurse me. Proffering
to go with me and introduce me to which I consented, and where I found
comfortable quarters for the next month, and where I was nursed, cared for
as tenderly as if I had been their child. His amiable wife was to me as
a mother.

When I arrived there and preliminaries for my stay all arranged, the
Doctor remarked "I shall have to give you something to make you worse before
I can determine what is the matter with you. "If you do" said I, "you will
certainly kill me for I feel I cannot bear much more now." By the next
morning, however, I felt better. The Dr. looked at me very carefully and
remarked "I know now what is the matter, you have got the measles". I
looked at myself in a glass and sure enough, I was as spekled as a turkey

egg. Here I remained until Bro. Mullins came around on his next
appointments. He had taken them from me, but only lay up about a week and
started round filling his appointments as usual. His attack was very light
and mild. I started out with him, who had left appointments for me, which I
met, and got round as far as Society Hill at brother Thompsons and was taken
down again, but revived in a day or two and went on again; and made out to
get around to Dr. Herberts again where I stopped a week. And in this way
during the whole year - preaching a little and laying up frequently, taking
medicine and not getting stout so as to do constant effective work at the
third quarterly meeting the brethern at Ebenezer (now Oak Hill) proposed
to the Presiding Elder Bro. John Boswell to give me a respite; this was I
think in July. Brother Richard Pipkin, a local elder, urging it on the
ground that I was not really able to work, I was trying to perform, consequently Bro. Boswell gave me leave to stop a while and try and regain my
health. After this I spent a week in Black's Bend, visiting the sick from
house to house, being a very sickly year particularly in that part of the
circuit. From this point, I went home to my Mothers accompanied a part
of the way by Brother Hearn. Remained there until about the first of
September and returned much improved. In the meantime, Bro. Mullins had
worked faithfully and had added many to the church. I took up my regular
appointment and laboured the balance of the year without much inconvenience.
We had that year an excellent Camp Meeting at Taits chapel, Black Bend,
where about forty five were added to the Church and numbers converted,
among them Bro. and Sister Theophilus Williams of Monroe County, two excellent members through life.

Soon after this camp meeting closed, Bro. Richard Pipkin who attended
it and preached acceptably was taken sick with fever at this home in
Allenton and died; and whose remains lie mouldering in the grave at Oak Hill.
I think the number taken into the church that year was about two hundred.
In company with Brother Mullens that fall we attended a camp meeting at
Simpson's Camp Ground, not far from Bellville. The Presiding Elder Bro.
Boswell was there and preached forcibly and effectively.

Here I formed the acquaintance of three worthy and efficient Local
Preachers. Lewis Pepkin, Joshua Peavy and Blanton P. Box of whom more
will be said hereafter. We returned back to our Circuit and the last
round we travelled together, preaching and exhorting alternately and
winding up the business of the year's labours, transferring and making

new class books; so as to leave matters properly adjusted for our
successors.

On this round at Dr. Barge's church, it was my time to preach. When
we got there (a week day) the congregation consisted of one white woman
and one black woman. We had taken our seats in the pulpit, I commenced
to look up my text. Bro. Mullens asked me, what are you going to do?
Will you preach to only two? said I, yes. "You get down there on one of
those seats and there then will be three, enough to claim the promise; and
I will do the best I can from the text 'Where two or three are gathered
together in My name, there I will be in the midst.'" Accordingly he took
his seat near the stand commenced singing, but happened to cast his eyes
at me and burst into a laugh and left his seat and came back into the
pulpit saying "I can't stand it, it looks too ridiculous." I commenced,
intending to do the best I could for the good white sister and the colored
one. But at the close of the prayer, Dr. Barge and wife, Squire Benson and
wife, came in so I had six, a pretty good week day congregation for that
place.

We closed up the work at Society Hill, Bro. Thompson's church, who
was the recording steward, and paid us our salary one hundred dollars
which was the disciplinary allowance to a single man. Besides this we had
been the recipients of several presents in the matter of clothing & c.
Particularly in socks from the good sisters. I never had as many pairs of
socks at one time before; which I took to conference and after selecting
from the bundle as many as I thought I would need, divided or gave the
balance to the young preachers who had not been as successful in this line
as I had been.

– An Incident On Our Last Round –

While passing through Blacks Bend, bidding the people farewell, both
black and white, a good old colored brother who had been a regular attendant
at our appointments, at Taits Chapel, was near the road at work in a field,
saw us coming and approached us, with something in his hand and thus addressed
us. "Well my young Massa's I 'spose you are going to leave us, sorry for it,
shall always 'member you and pray for you, hope the good Lord will be wid
you and bless you. Wish I had something more valuable to give you, but I
hain't; am poor; but if you will 'cept this from the old nigger it will
show you I love you and wish you well" At the same time handing each one
of us a nice roasted potatoe, saying "dis is all the old man has got".

Of course we accepted it with many thanks, and prayers for the good old brother. And I do not suppose that we had received anything in this way that we more highly appreciated than the good darkies potatoes; not that we needed them, but being a token of kind regards and the fruits of a benevolent heart and an evidence of love for those who had laboured for him in the things pertaining to another and better world, it was esteemed more highly than silver or gold.

This closed the labours of two young itinerants in 1834.

Being in the same class and having assigned to us the same studies upon which we had to be examined and passed in order to be admitted into full connection in the conference; and receive Deacon's orders, if the conference adjudged us worthy, we reviewed, read and examined each other on the different books designated while together this last round and after we left for conference at intervals when time and travel would allow. And be it remembered, that the young preachers study on those times consisted of horse back long rides, the woods, or private apartments of brethren's residences, where such could be procured at evenings and mornings before preaching. But principally his reading and study was performed in the saddle in his long rides from one appointment to another.

– Left For Conference at Greensborough –

On our way thither we stopped and spent the Sabbath with a brother Smith in the vicinity of Spring Hill. This was in the bounds of Marengo Circuit, which brother Mullins had travelled the year before. He preached at the church on Sunday where I met brother Thomas S. Abernathy who took me into the church in 1826 at Salem Camp Meeting as already noticed. From this point after visiting Demopolis, we proceeded to Greensborough. My lodging was assigned me as at Montgomery the winter before, with a crowd of young preachers, among whom was Walter H. McDaniel, Theopilus Moody, and others; in the upper room of an old building, the lower part of which was used as a machine shop for the putting up and sale of Spinning Jennies by a Mr. Peter McIntyre, taking our meals at a Brother Dickens, a prominent member of the church of that place. He entertained a number of the older preachers, Bishop Andrew among them. Here as before I had a violent attack of Asthma so bad that several of my associates, brother Moody particularly, thought I would die; and advised me to cease travelling and retire from the active service of the conference. This I was not willing to do and so continued; and what is the sequel? I am still here, brother Moody and most

of that crowd of young preachers gone. I do not remember all of them,
but know of but one who still survives and which is brother Walter H.
McDaniel, still an effective man in the Alabama conference. My class
consisted as the year before of Robert Smith, E. H. Moon, Robert
Dickson, Alex. Robinson, Humphrey Williamson, Isaac N. Mullins, Theophilus
Moody, Hugh M. Finley and myself. Brother Austin Davis who joined when
we did died the first year. All of whom were examined and passed, except
Bro. Moody, he was deficient is his studies and left on trial by the first
vote taken, much to his mortification, but the vote was afterwards reconsid-
ered; and he was received with the rest, elected to Deacon's Orders, which
was conferred by the imposition of Bishop Andrews hands the Sunday
following.

Brother P. F. Sterns had been stationed in Greensborough that year
and upon whom rested the labours of conducting the outside business at
this session, which he discharged, I think to the satisfaction of all. He
was the next year sent to the Chambers circuit where he married a Miss
Lane; and at the end of that year located and settled at Camden, Wilcox
County, Alabama and where he maintained for years his Christian integrity
and character of a good preacher, faithful and pious Christian gentleman.
He afterwards moved to Eastern Mississippi where I learn he still remains,
the same good Paul F. Sterns as before.

The close of this conference & entrance on the work of 1835.

The conference business having been completed, the Bishop gave us our
appointments to which we all soon repaired.

I was assigned in charge of Conecuh Circuit with James Shanks as my
colleague. Bro. Mullins to the Haynesville Circuit during which year he
married a Miss Mason and subsequently located.

And as I have taken the liberty to give a short sketch of my former
colleague, Bro. Foster and other brethren, with whom I was intimate and in
parting with Isaac, I must be allowed to say some few things of him. Bro
Mullins was a fine specimen of humanity; fine looking perhaps the peer of
the conference in this regard; healthy, of fine form, a good eye, and face,
erect in stature; commanding address in the pulpit; so much so I often
told him he was too popular, at least among the young ladies; his carriage,
appearance and address was too fascinating for his good and if he did not
watch closely, he was liable to be caught in a snare that might not be so

pleasant. Had an affectionate temperment; unsuspicious; judged people, particularly the ladies by their outward appearance and would often become enamored and fall in love with ladies on his first acquaintance. Which by the by was a good and amiable virtue and would have been more so, had it been mixed with a pretty good degree of caution.

As a preacher, above mediocrity, commanding generally good appreciative congregations, would have developed to some considerable distinction as a theologian if he had earnestly applied himself. He, however, made considerable improvements while I knew him and I, since learned that as a local preacher, he made advancements as an acceptable and efficient preacher of the Gospel.

After his location, he bought a farm and lots of negroes, mules & c near Mount Meigs in Montgomery County on a credit and engaged in farming. I spent a night with him on his farm in the Spring of 1837 and after giving me the details of his trade, his intentions, prospects & c, I at once advised him to give it up; get the man to take it all back, if he would, for my candid conviction was he would, never be able to pay for it by running it, which was his only chance, and which at the end of the first year he was compelled to do, by paying one years rent and paying for supplies for running it that year which involved him not making enough that year to meet these demands. The last time I saw him was at Summerfield years after when he told me he was just getting that debt paid off for that years farming. He studied medicine, became a doctor and lived a while in north Alabama, thence at Summerfield and finally moved to Texas continued to preach and practice medicine until a year or two ago, he died. From an obituary notice of his death in the New Orleans Advocate, I learned he established there the character of a worthy citizen, good preacher, successful doctor, a pious good man and died in the faith. So ended the career of my second colleague, whom I learned to love and admire.

   − The Conecuh Circuit and My Work On It In 1835 −

This circuit embraced a part of Butler, Conecuh, Monroe and Baldwin Counties; mostly in Conecuh and Monroe. The portion in Baldwin formerly belonged to the Baldwin Mission, and which was left that year to be supplied. But the Presiding Elder, not being able to engage a man for it, at my first quarterly meeting, it was suggested by some of the official members that I take it back into the Conecuh Circuit (at least as far down as Montgomery Hill) where it originally belonged. This met the approbation of the

Presiding Elder, I told them I could do so by making some changes in the
circuit so as to throw some rest days I had at other points into that part
of the work and supply the three appointments - Rhodes, Hendersons and Davis,
which met the approbation of all; thereby adding three more appointments
to my then hard circuit. These appointments were supplied that year as
many others on the circuit with work day preaching.

At this quarterly meeting the brethren gave me leave of absence to
visit my mother whose health was then fast declining. In company with the
Presiding Elder (E. Hearn) I proceeded on by Mobile, thence across to my
old home, found Mother declining, but left her and returned to my circuit.
Brother Shanks who had been assigned there to assist me, failed to come;
hence the whole burden fell on me. During the year brother John Sirmon,
a local preacher, filled one or two rounds. Except that the work was
supplied badly however by me, but I had an efficient corps of Local
Preachers who rendered much and valuable service; besides Brother Green
Malone, a superanuate, in the Alabama conference was with me, a considerable portion of the year and often assisted me. So that taking into
account all these agencies, I do not know that the works suffered. But
being in charge, I had trouble, several Church trials and what made it
worse mostly between the women. Two at Claiborne, one at Monroeville,
one at Long Creek, two of which were of a delicate character to be handled
by a young man. But I succeeded in getting them all out of the church.

One among many incidents occured here this year, that I will mention,
to show the motives by which some men are led to assume the very responsible position of a preacher of the Gospel.

There lived a brother on this circuit, who wanted to preach and the
church had given him license to Exhort. He met me at one of my first
appointments and I the next day accompanied him home in the neighborhood
of my next appointment. He conversed very freely on the subject of
wishing to obtain license to preach. Said he had no talent for exhortation, but had for unfolding the truths and doctrines of the Bible; that
his talent ran in that line, to explain and expound the scripture and
intimated that in some of his efforts where in he had called in question
some of Dr. Clark's views, that some one had told him he had given a more
satisfactory explanation than Clark and that he differed with Clark on
several points & c. Finally came to the point at which he was driving
and said, "I want you to bring my case before the church and procure a

110

recommendation for me to the next quarterly conference for license to preach." "Well," said I, " my brother I can do so, but are you certain God has called you to this work, would it not be as well for you to hold on awhile, exercise under your present exhorting license; you can read and explain the scriptures, as well as with license to preach; for I presume you recollect John preached many things in his exhortation." "Yes," said he, "but that don't suit me; for if it would do no other good, it would relieve me from doing public duty; such as working on roads & c for here this year, I was warned to work on the road and I didn't think I ought to work being an exhorter and didn't go; the overseer returned me and I had to pay a fine because I was not licensed to preach". "Well," said I, "if that is the motive that prompts you, it will be difficult for you to get license and I presume even to get a recommendation from your church provided this is known to them". I conversed privately with several of the members, with the class leader, a kinsman of his, who promptly advised me not to notice him any further on this subject as they would not endorse him and said he ought not have license to exhort; they were tired of his harangues & c. So I dropped my new applicant for preaching authority, and at the last quarterly meeting his license failed to be received and we got clear of him. He went off, some other denomination, and I suppose never done much good to himself or any one else.

I stopped one night at a good brothers house who had settled a new place, built a new split log house and after I lay down I never in all my life was so annoyed and bitten as I was that night with bed bugs. I did not sleep one minute, set up in the bed and with hands and feet killed, caught and threw overboard lots of them. There were several children lying on the floor just below me for whom I felt sorry, as I cast many on them, but I found they were used to it and they slept soundly. The next morning the sheets showed the sign of murders having been committed the night before.

The good sister at the breakfast table that morning asked me if I were troubled with night walkers that night; I told her yes, so much so that I had not slept a wink, that I never was so annoyed in my life. She very quietly remarked "that she intended to scald them and would have done so before now, but it was not the right time of the Moon." This was carrying "moonology" further than ever I had heard it before. I felt provoked at the poor woman's ignorance. And told her "my sister, if you will apply plenty of hot water, moon or no moon, you can kill them, what effect in the world does the moon have upon bed bugs, when

111

the weapons of death are applied. "Give up your notions about the moon
and go to work and scald their lives out of them". But my lecture
done but little good for two weeks after this, brother John Sirmon stayed
there and fared as I did, but I didn't go back there to spend another night
that year.

I never had such a year of annoyances. Church trials at three places;
chinces at another; fleas at another; and last but not least, Itch, at
another; so that I was miserably beset the whole year with first one, then
another of these pests. And what I had not learned heretofore of the
felicities of itinerancy, I came near, if not quite, graduating that year.

The flea case was on this wise. There stood an old church on the
side of the road leading from Pine Orchard to Claiborne called Mount
Zion, which was delapidated and almost forsaken, hogs had been sleeping
under it for months probably years. On one of my rounds, old brother
Nathan Sirmon accompanied me. We rode up to this house where I was to
preach that day, hitched our horses near the house, took off our saddles.
Soon I discovered our horses began to kick and move about, but gave it
no particular concern. Two ladies were sitting in the door. I took up
my saddle bags and walked to the door. Said they, if you don't mind you
will get fleas on you. There is lots of them here. We looked and saw
we were literally covered with them. I had a buffalo rug over my saddle
and my saddle bag covered at each end with bear skin, both of which
provided a good hiding place for them. I said to brother Sirmon, "Let's
leave here." "O, no,"said he, "not until we have prayers". "We must not
let the devil run us off with fleas." He had a prayer, but offered while
fighting and scratching. The poor sisters suffered, I know, as well as
we did. We left, went that evening to a brother Staceys, took the woods,
killed and knocked off many but they had crowded the bear skin, buffalo
rug, saddle and saddle blanket and even had penetrated my saddle bags
among my clothes until it was at least a week before we got rid of them.
I did not have another appointment at that house again. Moved the preaching place to brother John Stacey's house. They undertook finally to
destroy the fleas and they succeeded effectually by scattering pine straw
under the house, it being some distance from the ground, set it a fire,
which burned up the old house fleas and all.

The Itch

This miserable pest I caught some how or some where, I know not, but

caused me to lose a week or more lying up at brother John Sampey on a
blanket, greasing, rubbing and bathing with sulphur and lard until I
subdued it as I thought; at least got it under control so that I washed
and scoured up and started again, but it was not dead. Every little
pustule on my hands produced a large wart; and the next Spring I was
awfully afflicted with boils and warts, and had I have known what I learned the next year, to have taken the sulphur inwardly as well as apply it
outwardly, I believe I would have been entirely cured that year but more
on this subject in the next years chapter.

– The work on the Circuit & c –

This was attended to under all our discouraging and harassing circumstances to the best of our ability. And although there were not as
a general thing any great manifestations of revival power, yet at many
points conversions and accessions occured. And the membership considerably strengthened, peace and harmony prevailed, and the expulsion of some
of the dead branches appeared to impart new life and vigor to those alive.
During this year, I attended the marriage of Bro. Anthony S. Dickinson to
Miss Scotta Smith. The ceremony was performed by Bro. Green Malone. And
in the summer of the same year, I married my first couple, Mr. Richard
Sirmon and Miss Nancy Grace, and afterwards in the same community, my
second couple, Bro. James Wright to a Miss Pigot. Since then to the present
I have married more or less nearly every year, so that I presume it will
run up into the hundreds. Sorry I had not kept a memorandum of them and
the number of funerals attended & c.

We held one camp meeting that year at Simpson's Camp Ground; had but
few visiting ministerial brethren with us. Bro. Asberry Shanks from the
Cedar Creek Circuit was with us and preached very acceptably and I think
profitably. An incident occured connected with this camp meeting that may
not be amiss to mention, which shows the prevailing opinion of some of our
good brethren, that in order to have a successful and reviving meeting, it
is not only important but absolutely necessary to have the first talent of
the church, Doctors of Divinity and in a word, Big Preachers, so called.
Relying entirely upon the talent, the name, the standing of such, instead
of on God from whom alone vitality and power must be imparted to the Word
if good is accomplished whether that word be delivered by the great or the
more humble.

On this occasion, I had been importuned and teased by a brother to
write to Mobile and secure the aid at this camp meeting of Robert L.
Hennon who was stationed there and Robert L. Walker which I did; but
in reply both informed me they could not come. The evening we moved upon
the camp ground, in company with Bro. Shanks, who had arrived,we met this
brother; said he to me,"Did you write for Hennon and Walker?" "I did",
was my reply. "Are they coming?" "No," said I, "they wrote me neither
of them can come". "Well," said he,"we'll have no meeting. If I had have
known that I would not have tented. I believe I will go right back home."
This mortified me very much, coming out in such broad terms in the presence
of Bro. Shanks. I said to him "Brother the battle is not to the strong or
the race to the swift. God often uses the weak things of this world to
confound the strong & c and if we have a good meeting, which I believe
we will, God must bring it about and if we will look to God and not to men
we will be sure to be blessed." I know he was rather a slipshod Methodist,
and if he ever professed religion, he was woefully backslidden, hence I
exhorted him to go to praying and look to God and not to Kennon or Walker,
and he would see before the meeting closed that he was wrong. He held on
however, got nearer and nearer the stand as the meeting advanced and after
Bro. Shanks had preached a warm soul stirring sermon to which this poor
brother gave particular attention, mourners and I believe backsliders were
invited and who should be about the first to approach, but this brother.
Whether he was fully reclaimed or not, he said to me at the close "We have
had a fine meeting". "Yes," said I, " did I not tell you we would if our
reliance was upon God.

                    — The Local Preachers on this Circuit —

     Brother Lewis Pipkin, Joshua Peavy, Blanton P. Box, Joshua Calloway,
John Sirmon, William Murphy, Thomas Burpo and Newett Drew formed a band
of as pious, energetic, intellectual and useful workers and aids in the
cause of God as could be found in any Circuit or Country. And to whose
efficient labours the building up and success of the church in that and
surrounding country was greatly indebted. While there were among them such
as appeared to be set apart for the defence of the Gospel in successfully
combating error and defending the principles and doctrines of the Gospel,
as held and taught by our denomination, yet all were in the main good,
sound doctrinal and experimental preachers; and by whose aid, counsel,
and instruction, the writer of this was greatly assisted in his work this
year. And while he felt under obligations to many of them; but to none,

                                  114

more than the two just named, Viz: Lewis Pipkin and Joshua Peavy. And while he could say much more in commendation and eulogy each in detail, for their work and work sake, yet without crowding this sketch with seperate notices of this valuable corps of Local Preachers, what I have said of them in general may suffice. But I cannot pass by without giving some additional items of the two above named, without the least disparagement to the others or any intention of invidious distinctions.

- Lewis Pipkin -

Was advanced in life had been preaching a number of years, was licensed in South Carolina and after labouring there for some time, moved to Georgia and preached the Gospel there about 26 years, thence to Alabama, settled near Bellville, and laboured successfully for 30 years, when with his children he moved to Arkansas and lived and died near Mount Vernon church where his remains now lie in Nevado County.

Among the many with whom I have been associated, preachers or laymen, I have met with none who surpassed him in the true scriptural type of Christian and minister. He was a man of prayer, of meekness of devotion, and consecration to God. His life and pious example, blended with respectable talents and a thorough knowledge of scripture, rendered his labours, public and private, acceptable, useful, and impressive so that his praise was not only in the churches, but among the ungodly his name had in it a power, causing the remark often among them, "if Uncle Moses (as he was called in consequence of his meek and quiet spirit) doesn't get to Heaven what will be the fate of the rest of us." Beloved and respected by all who knew him, died as he had lived, honored and beloved. To me he was a friend, father and counsellor during my association with him, while on this circuit and at several meetings afterwards where it was my good fortune to meet him before he left for Arkansas. His end was peace.

- Joshua Peavy -

Was an uneducated man, commenced preaching in South Carolina when he could scarcely read; and it was said commenced to improve himself by using the spelling book. Being endowed with great natural powers, an investigating mind; retentive memory and indomitable energy in the acquisition of knowledge; that by strict and close application, he became one of the best divines in all that country. It was often remarked he was the most thorough and better posted man in Biblical knowledge and an intimate acquaintance with the standard works of Methodist theology,

115

such as Wesley's Sermons, Watson's Institutes, Fletcher's Checks and
Clark's Commentaries to be found in all the land. A brother local
preacher told me that year "that it was a treat to him to visit Father
Peavy that he was the best commentary he could find."

His manner of unfolding and enforcing Biblical truths were cogent,
concise and clear, evincing a perfect knowledge of the Bible in support
of any doctrine or proposition that he undertook to establish or illucidate.
Had a relish for controversy whenever he heard the doctrines of his church
assailed as the following incident will show.

During that year there came among us from the north a Universalist
preacher who got permission to preach in the Baptist Church near Belleville
and circulated through the community that he would preach on "Rich Man
and Lazarus" but more particularly on the passage "He lifted up his eyes
in hell" & c. Brother Peavy attended and heard him. At the close he
(Peavy) announced to the congregation that he would preach on the same text
in reply to the doctrine advanced there that day, requesting the attendance
of all and particularly the preacher. The time for this reply was two
weeks ahead, circulation was given to it through all that country so that
on the day appointed, the church, although a large one, could not accomodate
the congregation. Such a gathering had not been seen in that country
probably for years. Seats were moved out under a beautiful grove of shade
trees, the preacher mounted on a table or large box where he held them in
silence for two hours, reading from the Bible every passage or incident
bearing on the subject of the future punishment of the wicked; which
passages he had carefully marked in his Bible and read them for fear he
might not give them in the exact language of the text were he to attempt
a quotation from memory giving as he passed on a clear and lucid explanation
of each particular passage; its signification, and application as set
forth by Wesley, Watson and Clark. And wound up by arguments and reasons
for future punishment drawn from the nature of God and His law and man's
relation thereto.

The Universalist preacher was present, who took notes as Bro. Peavy
proceeded. Some of his adherents requested their man be allowed to reply
instanter, which was refused on the ground that this meeting was not
appointed for a debate, and as brother Peavy did not reply to him at his
meeting, the courtesy now could not be extended to him. He published a
very lame reply in his Universalist paper, but further than this we heard

116

no more of it. And I believe the doctrine was not advocated but by few.
The preacher finally gave up preaching it. Studied law, became a good
lawyer, married well and was a respectable and useful citizen.

Brother Peavy had a large family and the next year, I think, he moved
to Wilcox County on Gravel Creek near Mount Carmel Church, where he
afterwards died, leaving behind him one son, and now one grand son,
ministers of the Gospel, now in active service of the church,beside one son
William who was for some time a member of the Alabama Conference is now
dead and gone with his Father to his reward.

Brother Peavy as was expected died in the faith. The writer of this
preached a funeral sermon on the occasion of his death at the request of
his family, using the text "I have fought a good fight, I have finished
my course, I have kept the faith & c IITim. IV ch. v 7-8.
            - The Closing Up of This Year's Work -
I attended two camp meetings on the Cedar Creek Circuit, Shanks and
Haskew preachers in charge. One at Ebenezer camp ground near Allenton,
another at Hopewell in Brother McFarland's neighborhood; both good, successful meetings; at both of which I met many old friends and acquaintances of
the year before, much to my pleasure and gratification.

These were both new camp grounds, the first was erected on pub ic land
near Ebenezer Church in the neighborhood of Thomas Armstrong, Henry Stock-
man and others. During the meeting a man in the neighborhood, Cullen Cotton
went to Cahawba to the land office and entered the camp ground and on Monday
morning posters were stuck up around the place forbidding the removal of
houses, tents, lumber or any material put or connected in way with the
improvement of the place. What the final result was I do not now distinctly
recollect, but think the tenters disregarded his orders, and moved away
such as they needed. One thing, I recollect that man never prospered, was
looked upon with contempt, the land was sold for his debts for a nominal
price and finally fell into the hands of Samuel L. Jones and whose estate
or some of whose heirs still hold it.

After attending these camp meetings I returned and wound up the
business on the circuit preparatory for leaving for Conference, which was
to meet in Tuscaloosa,filled the remaining appointments and closed the
years work at Belleville. The Recording Steward, Bro. Box, in connection
with brother Willie Williams, another steward, paid me my salary $100.00.
Also the Presiding Elder his pro rata and presenting me with a fine

overcoat, I took my leave and wended my way, passing through Wilcox, and
thence to Bro. Hearns in Dallas, arriving there at the close of the
session of the Airy Mount Female Academy and accompanied several of the
young ladies from Mobile, who were now returning from this institution to
their homes; to the steam boat landing on the river in company with Miss
Lucy Hays and others, witnessing an affectionate leave taking between her
and the Mobile pupils, particularly the parting with Miss Mary Kennedy
both of whom in company with Bro. and Sister Hearn I had met at the
Ebenezer Camp Meeting.

Thence I proceeded towards Tuscaloosa stopping on Saturday at an
old friend, twelve miles below Bro. James Kirby, whose kind and
affectionate wife received me with open arms and an affectionate kiss.
This was the same family I lived a few months with on Pearl River where
I lost the Indian pony, an account of which I gave given on pages 88 and
89. They had now moved and settled in Tuscaloosa County hence our meeting
was to us all a reunion of old friendship and an enjoyable occasion;
rehearsing old scenes, and changes that had taken place with us, during
the long interval that had passed.

I remained with them until Monday morning, attended church on
Sunday and heard an excellent funeral sermon preached by Bro. E. V.
Levert on the occasion of the death of Father Massengale, father of
Leroy M. Massingale then a member of our conference.

Brother Kirby very kindly took care of my horse during conference and
returned him to me at the close in fine condition.

Monday found me at Tuscaloosa, where I met many of the members,
particularly, the undergraduates and committees ready for the annual
examinations. These were gone through with in due time so on Wednesday
conference convened. Bishop Soule presiding much to the satisfaction of
all.

I was comfortably quartered at the house of a good brother and sister
whose names I have forgotten. Brother Anthony S. Dickinson, my roommate.
My class had become depleted by the death of Bro. Robert Smith and I believe
by the location or transfer of one or two others. The certificate of
recommendation of Stephen F. Pilley for admission into the conference was
presented by the Presiding Elder from the quarterly conference of the
Chickasawha Circuit. Whereupon objections to his admission were interposed,
by some of the older members of the conference among whom was his Presiding

118

Elder. Upon the grounds first, that he, Pilley, had once belonged to a
theatrical company; that he was a good fiddler, loved fun and frolic and
that as a minister he could not exert much influence in those parts of the
country, particularly in Mobile, where he had formerly been engaged in
this kind of sport. Another objection was that he was a married man and
had now a wife and child, which was with some few of the old men of that
day, a very formidable objection. While it was admitted by those who
knew him that he was a good preacher, studious and guilty even in his
sinful days of none of those wicked and vicious habits of profanity,
intemperance & c; but there was that theatrical life, that wife and
child; these were enough in the minds of some to debar him. Unfortunately
the young brother had but few friends in the conference who knew him.
His Presiding Elder E. Hearn, who was against him; Theophilus Moody,
D. E. Barlow who had been with him that year once or twice and the writer
of this sketch. Brother Moody who had been his pastor that year and Bro.
Barlow advocated his admission earnestly. The Presiding Elder and others
against him, on the grounds already stated. I had never made a speech
in conference before but concluded I could not afford to see this brother
sacrificed on such altars as they had erected. Knowing him as I did, when
a sinner, when in the world, and also when and where converted, his Christian walk and character since the time I had taken him into the church;
together with the high order of talent evinced in his public and private
ministrations, I defended him then and there to the best of my ability.
First on the ground of his conversion that these elder brethren appeared
to me to be inconsistent in opposing him, for once being a sinner; as they
all had been themselves and probably done many things as bad, if not worse,
than acting on the stage, or playing the fiddle; and yet they professed to
be converted that by the grace of God their hearts and lives had been
changed from nature to a holy life and thereby acknowledged the efficacy
of divine influence and power in their own cases, but denied it to others,
to brother Pilley; that the religion of Christ that had made them new
creatures, was insufficient to accomplish the same in the case of this
brother. That the same power that had changed the Apostle Paul who declared himself to be the chief of sinners could not in these latter days
change the heart of an actor or fiddler. Hence they were ante Methodistic
in the position assumed. Of his conversion, I had not the shadow of a
doubt. An account of which I gave in this sketch on pages 126 & 127.

In the second objection, I tried to argue that having a wife and
child was no sin and I saw no reasons why we should debar those having
them already in possession and admit others without them, but would soon
marry and encumber the church (as it was urged in this case) with a like
charge. Hence I thought both objections groundless. And in the course
of my remarks said to the Bishop, that if he considered me worthy of an
appointment and colleague the next year, that I would as soon take brother
Pilley if left to my choice as any one untried. I have given here the
substance if not exact words of this my first effort at Conference speeches.
Brother Pilley was received, and as the sequel will show was my colleague
for two years, became an eminent divine and theologian, lived and died a
member of the Alabama conference.

     - My Mothers Message to Me at this Conference -

Such was the state of her health, that she had given up all hopes of
recovery and so communicated to me through Bro. Barlow with the request that
if I could not get a respite to come home and see her to ask for a location
so that I could be with her in her declining hours. This I made known to
the conference, when Bro. Hearn remarked to me,"Never mind Brother Ramsey
I will arrange that matter for you." I then knew or very correctly judged
my appointment would be the Leaf River Circuit on which she lived.

     - The Close and Departure from Tuscaloosa -

Appointments read out. Leaf River Circuit A. C. Ramsey and Stephen
Pilley, Elisha Calloway, Presiding Elder.

Soon I bid adieu to the brethern and the beautiful town of Tuscaloosa
and its intelligent and worthy citizens for the last time as I have not
been there since. Very soon I was on the road in the company with Thomas
L. Cox, appointed to the Chickasawha Circuit, both of which, mine and his,
lay near each other, to enter upon the - - Labours of 1836.

Believing the bonds and imprisonments might not await me, but knowing
that a very large circuit, hard rides, swollen rivers and creeks and many
privations and afflictions possibly were before me, it was with considerable
fear and anxiety that I plodded my way thither. Having been thus far in my
itinerant course assigned to circuits requiring much labour, spreading over
large tracts of country, but now on one far more extensive in area, and
beset with more obstructions and difficulties than any former one, could
but deject and cause despondency. Yet I tried to go forward in the fear
of God believing his grace would be sufficient to sustain me. And the hope

and prospect of meeting my dear mother before she died stimulated and much
facilitated my moments and reconciled me to anticipated hardships.

Brother Cox, my travelling companion, was in bad health, consumption,
consequently the long and hard rides we had to make were indeed injurious
to him and no doubt one of these at least hastened his death.

We had to cross the Bigby at Coffeeville, arrived some time before
sun down, too soon as we thought to take up for the night as told we could
get accomodations two miles from the ferry, but when we arrived there could
not prevail on the inmates of the place to take us in; but there was another
house, said they, two miles ahead, a Doctor, who would be sure to lodge
us. We plodded on now, dark; got to the Doctors, a German, I judged by
his brogue, "No! No!, me no keep public house, Me no keep hotel; me can't
let you stay. Go on the the Courhouse there you find a hotel." The courthouse was then ten miles distant, but we had to make it before we found
lodgings, calling at every house, insisting on the grounds of Bro. Cox's
condition, then almost worn out. We finally about ten o'clock at night
arrived at Washington courthouse and was carefully entertained by Col.
Frisby and lady with whom I had formed an acquaintance when on the circuit
there in 1833. Mrs. Frisby being a member of our church, we were treated
kindly and the next morning we left leaving our good wishes and blessings
on them both.

We proceeded on stopping at Brothers Myers, Webbers, and other
convenient places; and finally arrived at Bro. Peter Helvertson in the
neighborhood of Salem Camp Ground on Saturday evening. Brother Cox
preached at Salem on Sunday, as also did bor. Job Foster, his farewell
sermon, who was preparing to move to Texas.

Bro. Cox and I spent the night at Brother William Carters where I
had often passed many pleasant hours. Monday evening I left for Mothers;
not being able to reach my first appointments commencing so soon after
the close of conference, I went directly with Bro. Cox to his appointment
at Salem, thence to my circuit. Found Mother very low, but unwilling at
first for me to neglect work on the circuit, to take care of her, as she
was well cared for by my brothers. I remained about a week with her and
then left to overtake my appointments many of which had fallen through.

In due time Bro. Pilley, wife and child was on hand, ready to enter
itinerant college. Obtained board for his family at Bro. Willis Holders,
on the southern end of the circuit and commenced his work requiring
five weeks to accomplish a round and necessitating his absence from his

family that length of time every round. He travelled two weeks after me
and I three weeks after him.

The circuit commenced at Dwires bulff on the Pascagoula in Jackson
County, extending through that county into a portion of Greene; thence
through the eastern part of Perry, into Wayne through a portion of Clark;
and into the eastern and middle part of Jasper including the courthouse,
Paulding thence to Garlandsville in Newton County, where we turned southward through the western portion of Jasper, through the southeast corner
of Covington into Jones, through it into the western portion of Perry and
the eastern part of Hancock back into Jackson, the starting point.
Crossing and recrossing the following streams - Leaf River, twice or
thrice, Boguehoma, Tallahala, Tallahoma, Red, and Black Creeks besides
others which were often crossed by swimming our horses and sometimes
ourselves. Here was a circuit larger than presiding Elders Districts
are now, besides more difficult to travel.

NOTE: — I should have stated at the proper place that when I left
Brother Cox he was very feeble, and before he accomplished his first
round on his circuit, was violently attacked with hemorrhage of the
lungs and died. A suitable memoir of this good man is published in minutes
of the conference. Likewise of Robert A. Smith who died that year at
Elyton instead of 1835 as I elsewhere have stated.

My time not employed on the circuit, I spent with my mother who
continued to decline until the 8th of June, she died.

Unfortunately and to my great regret, I was not with her at the
time. When I left her, she appeared to be declining gradually, but thinking that I could possibly perform another round and make arrangements to
have the most of my appointments filled, having already lost a good deal
of time I submitted the case to her, who reluctantly consented and I left
but before I got half round she breathed her last. I have ever since regretted that I had not lost the whole round rather than have been away
from her bedside to witness her triumph.

1836

A continuation from Vol. No. 1 of incidents on that circuit Leaf
River in 1836.

There were no special out pourings of revival influence or
power - - no camp meetings; and protracted revival meetings, had not then
become fully inaugurated, as taking the place of Camp Meetings, as is now
generally seen; hence no unusual or extraordinary efforts were made looking

to this end; further than the usual ordinary services which were at most points regularly attended by the church members and good congregations and which resulted in a goodly number of conversions and accessions and hopes indulged that good was done.

Brother Pilley was as I had expected him to be, an excellent co-labourer, filling his appointments regularly and promptly, a hard student, improved rapidly, well received, and left the circuit beloved and respected. Never intimated a desire to return to the stage or the fiddle.

One little incident connected with his former love for this sport and a desire to test him on this fiddling question occured between us on one occasion while walking the streets in Paulding, passing a shop (I think a saloon) we heard within a fiddle. Said I, "Brother Pilley how do you feel now when you hear such things; do you feel like you would like to return to that kind of sport again?" "No indeed", said he, "further than this if I had hold of it and was disposed should like to learn that fellow how to use it for he knows nothing about it." Brother Pilley had a fine musical talent both for vocal and instrumental. And after his conversion and entrance upon the ministry, cultivated it in vocal music so that he not only made himself acquainted with the science but became an excellent singer.

During the summer of that year, I attended a two days meeting with Bro. D. M. Wiggins in Smith County in the Mississippi Conference, in the neighborhood of Bro. Flowers, where I met my old friend and brother Samuel Graves, with whom I first commenced preaching on this same circuit in 1832. This was indeed a pleasant coincidence to meet one, whom I loved so tenderly and had taken such pains to get me started in the work was indeed a perfect treat to my feelings.

On Sunday I was appointed to preach and took a chill just before the hour arrived for services to commence, and preached with a fever on me. God blessed me in the effort; blessed the people and we had a good meeting. There were present some indians, the first time I had ever preached to the red man, who appeared to be much interested, and gave particular attention to the word preached. After services were closed, the old chief, or the one who appeared to be in control of the rest brought them and introduced them to the preachers saying "they all Christians." having been instructed and taken into the church by the Missionaries to the Choctaws years before.

I went that evening in company with Bro. Graves to Richard Flowers'
where I suffered that evening and night, with high fever, but able next
morning to travel back to my circuit. Bro. Graves went with me and remained and preached for me at several appointments. We got to Bro.
Simpson's in Jones County where I was taken down and remained there
weeks until Bro. Pilley came around; overtook me; I was then convalescent
had worried through in the absence of Doctors, medicines or any remedies
(as they were not to be obtained in that country, not a doctor in forty
miles of me). Hence I had a severe time. A friend who visited me one
Sunday advised me to take sulphur as he had used it in similar cases in
his family successfully. I had but little confidence in the prescription
but concluded to try it. It had a fine effect in several ways not only
in producing copious prespirations, and thereby lessening the fever, but
completely relieved me of boils, warts and dregs of Itch with which I had
been infected the year before as I have stated in a former chapter.
I had upon my right hand about three dozen and near as many on my left,
some as large as a quarter of a dollar, seeded and growing besides
this pest, I do not recollect how many boils I had had the spring and summer before, but they numerous. As soon as I commenced improving, the
warts began to peel off, until finally ever one was removed, so that I
recovered finally from my attack of fever, got clear of warts, boils and
a perfect cure of the itch; and I attributed it all to the use of sulphur
which I took every day for a month or more.

When Bro. Pilley came round, I told him he must make some arrangement
to get me away from there as I was tired and I believed the good people,
with whom I had been confined so long, were tired also. Accordingly,
we heard that brother Robinson, an elderly Baptist Preacher owned a Gig,
a two wheeled vehicle. Brother Pilley called on him for the loan of it
to convey me down to Bro. James Fairs in the Dupriest neighborhood; who
very cordially let him have it. We started, he riding my horse and I had
his in the Gig, filling his appointments, as we went on. The first night
at Mr. Griffiths, my fever returned, but was clear next morning; on we
went to Timothy Welch's another fever, cooled off and the next night
we arrived at Monroe, and put up at Mr. Proctors; another fever higher
than the two others. That night it rained incessantly all night; a creek
to cross the next day. Bro. James Fair came in that night, and went back
home in order to send help to the creek to assist us over the next day

knowing it would be very high. Next morning my fever had abated and we
started again; got to the creek and although ordinarily a small one
and bridged, we found it at least fifty yards wide, the bridge afloat,
and brother Fairs help had not arrived. Bro. Pilley very deliberately
remarked"I'll get you over. Yonder is a foot log, do you think you can
walk it?" I told him I thought I could. So he unharnessed, stripped
himself, got into the shalves and waded into the bridge, hoisted on it,
which was afloat, but finally rolled it off on the other side, carried
saddles and baggage over on the log, and soon we were on the road again,
after swimming our horses at a ford below the bridge. We soon met
Bro. Fair with two or three negro men coming to our aid, but too late.

Brother Pilley returned the next day with the Gig to Bro. Robinson
with many thanks from me for his kindness and to resume his appointments.

I remained at Bro. Fair's a week or ten days; got clear of my fever
as I thought, and started again, but as before the fever returned the
first night and also the second, but I continued on in this way until I
arrived at my brothers where I lay up until I finally recovered so as
to be able to ride without throwing me back again.

During this time Brother William had married Miss Mary Fairley
daughter of Judge John Fairley and was living at our old homestead.
Brother Daniel was living there also with them, had not yet married.
Brother William soon after settled a place between Red Creek and the
coast which he improved and is still living at the same place, has
never moved; done well. His wife after bearing him nine children died
and since he had married again a Miss Sabra Davis; has been blessed with
two good wives.   - My Subsequent Movements -

I now resumed and filled some appointments on the circuit, went up
as far as Bro. Fairs and from there to camp meeting at Santee in Covington
County, in company with James and Alfred Fair, meeting there the Presiding
Elder Rev. John G. Jones, Stephen Herrin formerly of the Alabama Conference,
Elijah Steele and others. Here I was met by my brother-in-law, John T.
Longino, whom I accompanied home to see my sister and family; spent several
days with them and returned to my work on the circuit and filling out the
year.

On my last round I had with me Wesley G. Evans who was then commencing
the ministry; and at my last appointment I preached at his fathers, who
lived then near the coast. I gave Wesley license to Exhort. Since he has
continued to preach as a local preacher, has been true and faithful and an

acceptable and useful preacher. Still lives in that country; has been
married twice; his last and present wife was Sister Susan Carter, one
among the best, and most pious young ladies I ever knew.

During that year I married several parties to wit: Mr. John Reed
to a Miss Myers, Mr. Norman McLeod to Miss Dantzler; Mr. Hester to a
Miss Davis, Mr. Stephen Hester to a French lady, and Mr. Russel Bond to
a lady whose name I have forgotten, these last three took place about
or near the time of my winding up of my work and subjected me to long
rides being remote from each other, besides having to cross and swim my
horse across Red Creek twice if not thrice. I suppose I rode at least
one hundred miles to celebrate the nuptials for these three couples and
received as a reward for so doing two dollars from one party and nothing
from the other two. Mr. Reed the first I married gave me five dollars
and which had given me no trouble, or hard riding, being in the neighborhood of brother Fairs while I was there convalescing. Mr. McLeod's
was at one of my regular preaching places.

- Annual Conference -

This body was to meet at its next session in Mobile, January 4th,
1837 which allowed the preachers nearly a month over some of the former
conferences to remain at work on their respective charges, and as I had
lost considerable time that year by sickness, I continued until Christmas
preached my last sermon that day being on Sunday at Bro. Evans near the
coast on which occasion his daughter Middie joined the church. Bro.
Evans then confined to his bed with a disease that terminated in his death.

From this point I went in company with Thomas Evans to Mr. Seth Batsons
and married Mr. Russel Bond; thence to my brothers and fixed up for conference, arriving there in Mobile in due time for the opening of the session.
Found Bro. Pilley there who had preceeded me, in order to be in time for
his annual examination; and found him comfortably quartered in Dauphin
Street, at the house of a Bro. McBride, whose roommate had not nor did not
arrive and whose place I filled, much to my gratification, to be with
Bro. Pilley, besides cared for by such estimable Methodist and friends as
Bro. and Sister McBride.

Conference opened at the appointed time. Bishop Morris presiding.
The regular routine of buisness was attended to and dispatched by the
Presiding Office with care and fidelity to the satisfaction of those
concerned. I was now eligible to Elders orders, and having passed my
regular examination, when my name was called; character passed; and was
duly elected and on Sunday following, was set apart to that sacred office;

126

by Bishop Morris according the formula of the M. E. Church; in connection
with the following members of my class, to wit: Edward H. Moore,
Humphrey Williamson and Theophilus Moody. Only four of us now left out
of the ten that originally and at first joined the conference on trial.
Six of whom were admitted into this conference at Tuscaloosa four years
ago; and four, namely Robert A. Smith, Isaac N. Mullins; Robert Dickson
and Alexander Robinson were admitted in the Tennessee Conference and
transferred immediately to the Alabama; and became members of my class.
Now reduced to this small fraction by deaths and locations. Davis, Smith,
Finley and died. Mullins, Dickson and Robinson had located.

During this conference Bro. George W. Cotton from the Chambers
Circuit was taken sick with Pneumonia, at the house of Bro. Gascoignes
and died. Bro. Pilley and I were with him in connection with many
other brethren much of the time; and present to close his eyes and witness
the last struggle. He died in peace, leaving a wife and daughter behind,
then in Lafayette in Chambers County. He desired to make a will and the
task of writing it devolved on brother Gascoigne and myself; he commencing it and I finished it and became one of the subscribing witnesses which
necessitated my having to go the next Spring to Lafayette to prove it,
in order to admit it to record in the Probate Court of that County. The
good brethren of Mobile very kindly bore the expense of burial. Bishop
Morris preached his funeral from Col. 5th Chap., verse 3 and 4 "For ye are
dead and your life is hid with Christ in God; When Christ who is our life
shall appear then shall ye also appear with Him in Glory." After which
his remains were decently laid away in the cemetery of that city where
they remain awaiting the Resurrection of the dead.

When the appointments were given us at the clo: by the Bishop I
was as the year before only to a different Circuit. And while it was
gratifying to me, nevertheless, a little surprising that Bro. Pilley and
I were kept together for another year, but so it was announced.

Cedar Creek Circuit: A. C. Ramsey and Stephen Pilley, Elisha
Colloway, Presiding Elder. Very soon now there was seen a rush among
the preachers getting off to enter upon their new fields of labour.
Brother Pilley returned to his mother-in-laws for his family; while I and
several others steered our course across the Bay in a little steam ferry
boat to Blakely where we with our horses landed, late in the evening,
spending the night at or near that place in the company with Zacheus
Dowling and Wilson Langley. Next day we separated, Bro. Dowling to the

127

right in direction of his circuit which lay eastward, while Bro. Langley
and I continued the main river road leading to Claiborne, stopping that
night at Bro. Davis near Montgomery Hill, one of my stopping places,
when on the Conecuh Circuit in 1835. We had in our company also Bro.
Lewis Stephen Pipkin of Bellville. I met here at Bro. Davis a young lady
there on a visit from Dallas County ony my circuit. Miss Lucy Hays with
whom I was well acquainted and whose name is mentioned in a former part
of these sketches. Her society and that of Miss Elizabeth Davis together
with the entire family rendered my sojourn there that night quite a
pleasant and agreeable one.

The next day Saturday, we passed through Claiborne, and took up at
Bro. Theophilus Williams six miles above, where we spent the Sabbath. In
this family I had spent many pleasant hours and happy seasons in 1833
the year I travelled the Conecuh Circuit. And was by them in the altar
at the Blacks Bend Camp Meeting in 1834 when they were both converted.
Hence our meeting again was not only pleasant but affectionate and
profitable. Sister Williams was an affectionate, pious woman; quite uncommon to her, at church, that under the preaching of the word her soul
did not become stirred to such an extent that she often gave way to her
feelings in exclamations of joy. She also carried her religion home
entering into all her daily walk and conversation. She finally lost her
mind and while she was unable to converse intelligibly on the common topics
of every day life; but let the subject of religion be mentioned, her face
would at once become a glow; her eye radiant and conversation fluent and
sensible. Good meetings were her general theme; she loved them, when
sane and now they occupied her thoughts to such an extent that even while
deprived of reason, the Good Lord cleared her mind and unlossed her tongue
upon the subject of the Salvation of her soul. She died a few years ago,
after thus suffering for many years. "And while she now rests from her
labours, her works follow her." Bro. Williams was a pious good man after
he embraced religion. Consistent in his professions, life and deportment,
a useful citizen, efficient church member, raised in respectibility a large
family of children, most of whom were married before the death of Sister
Williams. He died a few years ago and from his professions and life, we
have hope in his death.

The next day after leaving brother Williams, I got to my circuit
and stopped at Bro. John F. Davis and entered upon

Editor's notes:

Page 122 - Dwire's bluff - Daniel Dwire had land on the Pascagoula River as early as 1811.

Page 123
Bro. Flowers - Richard Flowers of Covington County, MS

Samuel Graves - lived in Copiah County, MS

Page 124
Brother Simpson's in Jones County, Nathan or Nathaniel Simpson

Brother Robinson, an elderly Baptist Preacher - Norvell Robertson of Covington County, MS. Bro. Robertson also left a diary or his memoirs in the form of an autobiography. Norvell Robertson was born in Virginia in 1765; served in the Revolutionary War, migrated to Georgia where he married Mrs. Sarah Powell in 1791. He emigrated to Mississippi in 1816, along with Stephen Cranberry and William Albritton and George Cranberry; Seth and Moses Cranberry; Allen Coward.

James Fairs in the Dupriest neighborhood of Perry County. The name here is Farr, rather than Fair. The Farr's and Dupriests were related James Farr and Alfred Farr lived near the Dupriest in Perry County and James Dupriest was married to Penelope Farr, sister of the Mother of Alfred Farr. There is a lawsuit in Hancock County, MS in 1859 involving the Farrs and Dupriests. Delilah Farr was the mother of Alfred Farr.

Mr. Griffith - This would be in Jones County. A. G. Griffith from North Carolina and his sons, Charles F., Johathan Eli, and William Griffith all lived in Jones County at this time.

Timothy Welch was an old settler in Jones County.

Page 125
Brother Fair - James Farr of Perry County, MS

Alfred Fair - Alfred Farr of Perry County, MS

Wesley C. Evans probably the son of Thomas Evans of Hancock Co., MS

Page 126
Susan Carter daughter of William Carter and Mary Goff.
Wesley Evans first wife was Amelia Woodruff.

Marriages performed by A. C. Ramsey.
John Reed to Miss Ann Myers
Norman McLeod to Millicent R. Dantzler

Bro. McBride on Dauphin Street - The Mobile City Directory for 1837 lists J. F. McBride as an undertaker and is the only McBride listed on Dauphin St.

Brother Gascoigne - Charles Gascoigne, a commission merchant who lived at 96 Government St., Mobile, Al.

Page 124

Mr. Proctor - Farr Proctor who was married to Margaret Dupriest. Judging by his given name, there is a possible Farr relationship also.

Commencing in Blacks Bend I went round meeting the first appointments,
(but at what point they commenced I do not now recollect) but found the
circuit in the same form I had left it in 1834, embracing the same territory
and same appointments, no particular marks of aggression in point of new
appointments, accessions to the church or any great increased development
of spiritual piety, yet quiet and harmony appeared to prevail. Some
pruning had necessarily been done by our venerable or worthy predecessors
so that upon the whole the church appeared to be lying on its oars neither
advancing or retrograding to any considerable extent, but merely holding
its own. And in this condition, it remained at several points during the
year; at other points good meetings, revival influence appeared to prevail
and accessions to the church were marks that some good was accomplished
that year.

When I got around to Greenville, I met brother Pilley with his
family who accompanied me on my round to Oak Hill (then Ebenezer) near
Allenton.

We obtained board for his family on Oak Hill at brother John
Sampeys who lived there at this time. But by the first quarterly meeting
circumstances rendered it necessary that another boarding place must be
had. Whereupon Brother Calloway came with me to Oak Hill where we found
the Recording Steward, brother Willie Williams, had taken charge of
Brother Pilley and family until another could be secured. There were then
no parsonages, no place for the preachers family and stewards generally
neglectful or forgetful of their duties and brother Pilley's salary was
about $224.00 if it could be collected and the stewards made no provisions
for paying house rent or board; so that it looked at one time rather squally
for Bro. Pilley. But he came there to preach and if God would help him,
he intended to worry it out, and accomplish the object of his mission which
he did. And further I saw Bro. P. tried, the more I became convinced that
he had a right ring of itinerant metal and that success would attend such
indomitable energy and nerve embodying with it such patience, meekness
and submission to hardships that I felt I was right and God would and had
sanctioned the effort I made in getting him into the conference; and which
his subsequent life and labours contending with poverty, toil and affliction has fully vindicated.

I now proposed to Bro. Pilley and Presiding Elder for him to go with

me on my round and I thought I could get him a place; so accordingly
it was agreed to and when I got as far as brother Barns on Flat Creek
we obtained board with him for the year, where he was taken care of
and filled the years work. At this place during that year his son
Stephen Abiezer was born, conferring on himself and me the honour of
giving the son his own and my name. Who grew up and under God became and
is now an eminent and useful minister of the Gospel, a member of the
Alabama conference and hence I consider it no disgrace or discredit to
either name.

Brother Pilley lived to raise a large family of children; three of
his sons ministers of the Gospel and one daughter married a minister
(Bro. Selman). He finally became diseased and died a few years ago a
superanuated member of the Alabama Conference. The children became some
what scattered but the most of them with his widow live in Butler County
where he died.

- Brother Daniel's Marriage, Life & Death -

He was my youngest brother who with brother William had remained
single, taking care and providing for Father and Mother in their declining
years and nursed them both until they died and now as the connecting link
that bound them to the old homestead was severed; it becomes necessary
that they should secure another link that would bind them to homes of their
own; accordingly (brother William had already married) on the 12th of
February of this year 1837, brother Daniel was married to Miss Mahala Holder,
daughter of Willis Holder then of Jasper County, Mississippi, a part of
the history of whose life has been already noticed in these sketches. He
settled in that country where he was brought up and in which he spent his
life;became pious and a useful citizen and member of the church, accumulated
property and raised a family of nine children all of whom are grown and
married and considerably scattered. One in Missouri, one in Texas, two in
in Alabama and the balance at and near the coast where he died, which
occured at his home at Bell Fountain in Jackson County, Miss where he
was buried in 1867.

But I must return to my work on the circuit. This was attended to by
driving and labouring to the best of our ability at the different appointments, twenty or twenty one every four weeks and at several places
during the year, there were accessions, conversions and the signs of an
onward and upward movement. Bro. Pilley was very acceptable and useful

131

losing no time, but devoting himself wholly to his work. So at the close
of the year we had reasons to believe some good was accomplished. One
important event in my history occured with me that year. On the 4th day
of August, I was united in marriage with Mrs. Elizabeth Amanda Bonham, a
widow with four children, a fearful and responsible undertaking I knew,
but 'e it was, I voluntarily assumed the position, influenced I think by
no other motive than a pure affection for the object of my choice and
probability of placing myself in condition to be able from declining
health to be more useful; to do more good to the cause of Christ and my
fellow man than I otherwise were doing, or could do; I selected her and
the position with the knowledge and apprehension of the dangers involved;
subjecting me to the misjudged opinion of many at the time, that mercen-
ary or sinister motives were the ruling principle that governed my action.
Yet while I was aware that probably I might incur burdens and responsibilities, too great for me in caring for her and her children, managing a
business with which I had but little acquaintance and thereby make a
failure and bring upon me the abuse and anathemas of those who were
intimately connected by ties of relationship with the family; besides the
slander and gossip of others. I, of course, feeling conscious of the
honesty of my motives could but enter into such an alliance with fear and
trembling. But believing and knowing that I should have the aid of a
woman of sense, of principle, of management care and industry and the best
of all, one of devotion and affection for me, I married her and took charge
of her business and which I so managed afterwards, I believe, in every
instance as to not only meet her approval, but likewise the approbation
of her friends and those more directly interested in its proper adjustment.
And while I had many annoyances, and much harassing labour to perform and
scenes to pass through, I found her as I expected her to be, a helpmate,
a loving, sympathetic companion through life. Among one of the most
domestic, careful, business housekeepers I ever knew. She was a religious
woman, never opposed me, in going where I thought I ought, to preach, or
to attend to any work connected with the church to which I was called; but
was to her a great pleasure to know that I was trying to do all I could
for the cause of Christ.

    She lived to be the mother of seven of my children, and after
suffering for a considerable length of time died June 3d, 185.. at our
home at Oak Hill in Wilcox County, Alabama where her remains now lie in the
graveyard at that place. Gave satisfactory assurances in her affliction
that her peace was made with God and had a bright hope of Eternal Life.

And before leaving this subject I wish to say right here not in
a boastful or self applauding spirit, but in the fear of and reverence for
God and with profound gratitude to his watchful care over me; to his
sustaining grace vouchafed in and through the very many trials, temptations,
changes and cares through which I was called to pass, by assuming the
change of a single life to one of taking care and watching over the inter-
ests of a large family, in becoming parent or guardian of children that
were not my own together with the almost incessant tax upon mind and
thought that in all this I can say conscientiously I never forgot my
obligations to God or at any time sacrificed my religion either in faith
or practice but at all times whether in sunshine or shade endeavored to
maintain my religious integrity and standing as a minister of the Gospel
labouring and acting with an eye to God's glory and the salvation of the
souls of those over whom I had the charge as well as to all others with
whom I came in contact. And now believe I can say that my usefullness
as a Christian and minister was not diminshed but rather increased by
my marriage and to which I think many who know me before and long afterwards will testify.

The regular work on the circuit was attended to promptly, the
balance of the year. At the close of which, I attended the conference
which convened at Columbus Mississippi January 3rd, 1838. My trip to
this conference was rather a novel one, in company with Rev. E. Hearn,
who had previously gotten a fall from his horse and fractured a leg.
Such was his great anxiety to attend the conference, having now missed one,
that he determined to go although could not walk on his limb, used crutches
altogether. We started and made the trip on horse back; I having to assist
him on and off his horse at ferries and stopping places, which was rather
a laborious task. But we arrived in time although the conference was in
session, presided over by Bishop Andrew. Here as at the conference the
year before, another of our good and great men died.

                    - Rober L. Kennon -
was taken sick soon after his arrival with Pneumonia and the day the
conference closed he died. A great loss to the conference and church.
When his death was announced in the conference room, Bishop Andrew suspend-
ed business for a while when a general weeping prevailed through the entire
body. Brother Kennon was regarded as the Father of the Conference, his wise
counsels, pious walk and loving spirit attached him to all, but especially
to the young preachers to whom they were greatly indebted for the tender
and fatherly care exercised by him in their examinations, and for many

valuable lessons of instruction given them by this man of God. He was to
the conference and the church, a Beacon light. Dr. Kennons name will be
cherished and remembered by many generations following him. And when the
historian shall write up Methodism in Alabama his name, his life, his
usefulness, his talents and his labours and toils in planting her standard
will form one of the most conspicious chapters. His remains were conveyed
to Tuscaloosa, Alabama where they were interred and where they lie awaiting the resurrection of that last day. Thus by a strange and mysterious
Providence, our ranks had been deprived of two good men during the sittings
of the Conference, George W. Cotton, the year before and Dr. Kennon at this
conference. Since that time the same coincidents have occured at subsequent conferences. Rev. Ebenezer Hearn, Dr. Jefferson Hamilton and A.
McBride who died on the cars soon after leaving conference at Auburn,
Alabama at which Rev. E. Hearn was taken sick, but was removed to
Montgomery where he died. After this in 1872, Dr. Hamilton while at
Conference in Auburn (Opelika), also died.

- My Request of the Conference -

Such was the state of my declining health, my Asthma increasing,
and subjecting me to much suffering, augmented by the long rides, exposure
and labour on the large circuits I had been on, that I saw location with
me would be at no distant day inevitable; and in fact some of my brethren
before this knowing the severe sufferings I had to endure adviced me to
stop, but this I did not wish to do, but now as I had changed my life and
gotten me a home, I considered it duty to make a change, but did not ask
for location, but only to be left without an appointment that year, so that
I could rest and probably, be better prepared to do effective work thereafter. This request was granted and I had no work assigned me by the
conference for the year 1838, but laboured mostly as much as formerly
although in a more limited sphere.

Brother Daniel Monaghan and Bro. Mills were appointed to Cedar Creek
Circuit this year, with whom I laboured and assisted them in their work.
This circuit was well supplied with local preachers, I found on it the
year before, and also this year, the following, viz: James King, James
Thompson, Hazlewood B. Parish, Joshua Peavy, John Herrington, John Millis,
Paul F. Sterns, William M. Cracken and Peter Williamson. Three of which had
once belonged to the conference, in the travelling connection, but had
located to wit: Peavy, Parish and Sterns. The others had been local all

134

the time. And as I have already noticed in former sketches, some of these brethren, particularly bros. Peavy and Sterns, and as it would be crowding these sketches to too great an extent to be interesting to any to take up separately and give details of each one, I shall only remark in general terms; that there were but few circuits, if any, in Alabama blessed with as many preachers of this class that could surpass old Cedar Creek in point of talent, piety, labour and usefullness; some few excepted of course. Connected as they were with their domestic business, getting nothing from the church as a remuneration for their services, having to labour for a sustenance for themselves and families and contributing largely and annually to the support of the church and the itinerant preachers on the circuit, the wonder is that they maintained their ministerial integrity and were as useful as they were. But this they did, and through and by them, in addition to the regular preaching which they performed the finances of the church were annually augmented to such proportions that the various demands made upon the church would have been meager indeed but for their liberal contributions.

But without saying a word in disparagement to any, I must note a few items in reference to Father King and Brother Thompson.

My first acquaintance with the former was at Ebenezer Church at my first appointment in 1837. From that time until the spring of 1869, I was intimately associated with him. Was a close sound logical and useful preacher. On the terms of the law he had liberty and power. Loved to preach. Not a man of great variety, but such subjects as he handled had matured them well. His private life above reproach. In some things peculiar, but whose piety no one doubted, respected, loved by all. Lived to a good old age. Had been a local preacher about sixty years, died a few years ago at Allenton, Alabama and was buried at Oak Hill Cemetery by the side of his wife who had preceeded him to the better land, leaving behind him the odor of a correct life and pious death.

— Rev. James Thompson —

Was no ordinary man. Intelligent, sedate, pious and upright in his intercourse with others, always exhibiting the dignity of a Christian gentleman. As a preacher few could surpass him in the selection, preparation and delivery of his sermons often on certain subjects sublime; arising to such a point that the pathos, the mellow intonations on voice, coupled with the grand thoughts and arguments put forth that his congregations were often

so moved as to show forth in their emotional natures and other evidences
that they felt the power of truth stirring their consciences and finding
a lodgement in their hearts and minds.

Brother Thompson was a useful preacher. Never idle, preached a
great deal, his praise was in all the churches. It was my good fortune to
become acquainted with him early in 1834, when I was first appointed to that
circuit. From which we were together more or less every year except 1836
and an intimacy, friendship and affection grew up between us such as I
now love to cherish. Our associations were frequent at quarterly meetings,
camp meetings and protracted services besides our frequent visits to each
others homes. Hence I knew him well in private as well as in public life,
and can say that to know him was to love him; and I have met with few for
whom I cherished a greater veneration than James Thompson. His first wife
died in 1835, a good woman, leaving him six children. He married again
in 1836, a Mrs. Mason and was fortunate in getting a good woman to act as
mother to his children. He and all his children are dead. His remains
with the most of his children lie in the grave yard at Society Hill Church.

During the latter part of the summer of this year, I atended a
quarterly meeting of brother Calloway's at Suggsville on the Tombigby
circuit, in company with brothers King, Thompson, and McCracken. We
arrived there on Saturday evening, found several brethren in attendance
besides the Presiding Elder and A. S. Dickinson, P. C. On Sunday under
a sermon from Brother Thompson from the text "There is joy in the presence
of the Angels of God over one sinner that repenteth & c the spirit of God
moved the people, the work broke out and we continued for ten days and I
do not remember now of our attending a better meeting; one where the work
was more general, conversions more satisfactory and where the preachers had
better liberty in dispensing the Word of Life and when we closed the
second Sabbath of the meeting, left a large number of penitents at the altar.
I also attended another meeting with Bro. A. S. Dickinson at the Lower
Peach Tree, where we had quite an interesting meeting. Beside there I
assisted the brethren at several other points. So that although I was
left without an appointment that year, I was not idle and laboured as
much as my strength would allow.

                    ─ The Next Conference ─

Was to meet at Montgomery January 2d, 1839 which I did not attend yet
the conference granted me a supernumary relation and appointed me to labour

on the Cedar Creek Circuit that year in connection with Bro. L. B.
McDonald, preacher in charge.

(Note) - - I should have stated as transpiring in 1838, the birth
of my first daughter Jane Perrin, which occured May 13th, 1838. And in
the fall of the same year our trip to Abbeville District, South Carolina
accompanied by Jesse Calvert of that District, who had been travelling
in Alabama for his health. This was an afflictive trip. The night before
we arrived at Abbeville, my wife was taken sick with fever which continued
to increase until it became a violent attack, so much so we despaired for
a time for her recovering. A few days aft r I and our babe, Janie, were
also taken down and shortly afterwards our nurse, the negro girl, we had
brought with us was also taken sick from which she never recovered, started home with her in December, but had to leave her in Georgia on the way,
where she died. Through the hand of a kind Providence and the attention
of Drs. Joseph Wardlaw, my wife's brother, and Dr. Reed, we all finally
so far recovered as to be able to travel and after having been there confine
for nearly three months, we left for home by private conveyance bringing
with us from school there my wife's two eldest daughters, Hannah and Ann.
My wife was very weak and feeble, so much so as not to be able to sit up
in the carriage long at a time and consequently I procured a spring wagon
(called then a Jersey waggon) and mattress on which she could rest herself
and in this way we made the journey being on the road two weeks and
arriving home a few days before Christmas, much to our joy and delight
and especially so to the two youngest children, Bessie and Mamie, which
we had left in care of Mr. and Mrs. Richard Williams. My wife's health
had improved somewhat by the change and travel and finally recovered. Janie
was still sick and had that winter and the next sping, a long distressing
time caused by the debilitating effect of her South Carolina attack,
connected with such diseases as often follow "teething" so that her life
was dispaired of for some time. I tried many remedies among which was the
Steam Doctor practice administered by Dr. Herrington and which as I
thought done her more harm than good, and I finally gave up all medicine
and let her eat whatever she craved, buttermilk and potatoes particularly,
from the use of which she had been deprived by the Doctor. She at once
commenced mending and finally recovered.

I had become engaged in farming and consequently had to devote a part
of my time to that business, but during the year assisted Bro. McDonald

on the circuit filling regular appointments and several rounds on the
circuit and was instrumental in getting up a camp meeting at Ebenezer,
a new camp ground, where we subsequently held three other camp meetings
annually. Here at this first one, an incident occured which will do no
harm to mention.

Frederic J. Nosworthy, at one time a member in good standing in the
Georgia conference, and regarded as one of the best preachers in that
country but who had acted badly and was expelled from the conference and
church had moved into the bounds of that circuit in a backslidden and
wicked condition, but during the year of 1837 while brother Pilley and
myself were on that circuit, professed to be reclaimed and wished
license to preach, applied at the last quarterly conference of that year,
but failed; but the next year applied again, and succeeded; that conference
being held in his own neighborhood, and at his own church, remote from
the one the year before when his application was rejected, and in the
absence of those brethren who had apposed it, such as Brothers Peavy,
Sterns, Thompson and others. Under this authority he commenced preaching
and to do him justice, I must say he was one among the most effective
preachers I have ever heard; one of more power over the minds of his
congregations, than any I had ever known; travelled throughout the circuit
and adjoining circuits, producing great effects and results. Yet, not
withstanding all this, he was an unguarded man in his intercourse with
society. His old habits and passions appeared still to exert on him an
influence derogatory to the ministerial character; got in trouble again,
but was sustained by a church court, as not being guilty, yet in the minds
of some a different opinion was entertained; he attended this camp meeting.
Bro. McDonald had charge, but had transferred the control of appointing
the preachers to occupy the stand at the different hours to Father King.
Brother Asbury Shanks who was a Georgian and knew Nosworthy's history there,
besides being familiar with the recent difficulty in which he had been
involved attended this meeting in company with a large delegation from
Selma where Bro. Shanks was stationed that year, of men and women, who
declared positively "if Nosworthy was put up to preach, they would not
hear him". Bro. Shanks told this to Father King, who did not know what to
do as there was a great clamor from others for Nosworthy to preach. Hence
he was held off until Sunday at 3 o'clock P.M. when Father in consultation
with others decided to appoint him for that hour. Saying it was not right

138

to ignore the wishes of a large majority to please the captious whims of
a few Selmanites that if they did not wish to hear him they could stay
away. The appointment was made known to them. Several put up at my tent,
which was near the stand. They told me they would not go out, but I noticed
took their seats in the passages of the tent where they could hear distinctl
Shanks took his seat in the altar fronting the speaker. They had all been
told if they would hear Nosworthy he would be apt to preach down all their
prejudices. The preacher arose and in his opening prayer appeared to get
under the cross. In his appeals to God for help this one time any one
could readily see that he felt the importance of the hour and upon the
effort now before him, there was much depending, that in addition to
religious or moral results in the congregation which he prayed earnestly
should be produced, but the vindication of his own character, the removal
of settled prejudices against all hung upon the effort of the hour. He
announced his text "I pray not that thou shouldst take them out of the
world, but that thou shouldst keep them from evil." John 17-15.

He had not proceeded far before it was apparent that he had the
fixed attention of Bro. Shanks and a few of his Selma folks, who had taken
their seats in the congregation. He soon began to rise in the warmth and
ardor of his feelings in discussing his first proposition that there was
evil in the world, referring to its different phases and effects, and from
one point to another, soon became sublime and eloquent, throwing all the
pathos and emotion of his nature into his arguments and gestures, producing
evident marks that he not only had attention but the sympathy of his
congregation. I soon heard from Brother Shanks audible responses and there
by knew that Nosworthy had him. The others at the tents began to move
their chairs nearer the stand, and when he closed they were in the crowd
around the altar. He closed with a general shout to the congregation and
many penitents at the altar, many of whom found peace that night. Such
an excitement had not been seen or realized during the meeting. When we
retired to the tents I asked some of the good sisters "what they thought
of Bro. Nosworthy now?" Why, said they, He certainly must be a good man.
He certainly is persecuted, and whether he be a sinner or not, he can out
preach any man we have heard lately and in future, says one old lady, I'll
hear him every chance I have hereafter. Why, said she, he has completely
preached down all my prejudices. Bro. Shanks said,"What a pity that man
had not have done right through his ministerial course. What a power he

would have been in the church." "While listening to him I tried to lay aside
every opinion I had formed and really enjoyed his sermon, felt its truth
and weight, but for the life of me I can't help feeling and fearing that
he is at heart a bad man." Which really was the fears of all who had been
intimate with his history. Poor man, he had a rough road to travel; finally
left Dallas county and moved to Tallapoosa where he died and it was said
of him he gave evidence in his last sickness on his dying bed, that God was
with him in his forgiving mercy and he was ready and willing to go. I
recollect of making this remark, when I heard of his death, "That if he was
prepared and is gone to Heaven, it was better for him and the church too,
that he died". This may have been a wrong conclusion in me, but when I remember the troubles he had in his temperament and passions, which too often
got the control of him, of his better judgement and thereby led into acts
that not only gave him great trouble, but often in moments of calm reflect-
ion many regrets; and sometimes opened up avenues for other offences in
trying to vindicate himself from crimes of which he was charged. Hence
from these troubles he is saved, if he was prepared for death. As also
the church is relieved of a brother which she had to bear, by his wayward-
ness, and want of self government not only in the disgrace brought upon
her in Georgia, by his incautious conduct, but also in this country to some
extent by the indulgence we often feared of the same passions that terminated his ruin in Georgia and likewise of a reckless disposition to be in
company from home, neglecting the temporal wants of his family & c. These
and other reasons called forth the expression of the opinion above stated.

- Centennial Year -

Methodism was now one hundred years old. Or that length of time had
elapsed since the Methodist Church was organized. And the church in Alabama
desiring to present to God a thank offering for the watchful care over her
for the prosperity which under Him had marked and attended her this term
of years, and for that influence and power which she had through her
divinely appointed agencies exerted on the minds and hearts of the thousands
to whom she had ministered at home and abroad; determined to show forth
their gratitude and praise by contributing a fund and employing it in a
substantial way as a memorial of their appreciation and remembrances of
their obligations to Him who had thus blessed them. And believing that this
object could not be attained or accomplished in any better way where the
interest and well being of the Church could be better subserved and from

140

which more lasting good could be derived than to appropriate it to the establishment and building up at some convenient point an institution of learning for both sexes. To be of such a grade and order that all the academical and collegiate privileges and requirements could be obtained within its precincts and departments, so that to generations following our children could point to this sacred spot and not only behold the munificense of their parents in thus providing for their intellectual as well as religious wants, but exlaim "I was born there; I was educated there. Consequently, Summerfield was the spot selected in Dallas County where an Academy had been established for many years, which if I mistake not was now turned over to the church free of cost. The place now assumed the name of Summerfield instead of Valley Creek Academy. The institution was however designated as the "Centennary Instute of the M. E. Church" and since the division of the church in 1844 is the M. E. Church South.

The money necessary to carry out this enterprise had to be obtained by contributions from the people at large. Hence subscriptions were opened in every town, city and circuit. The preachers on their different charges were the appointed canvassers and collectors. Brother McDonald and I were the agents on our circuit. We went to work and soon had a nice subscription and collected it up and turned it over to the proper authorities. Others done the same, and very soon the work commenced and was advanced to completion as early as the means would allow. The Trustees were active in getting the buildings ready and very early had the Institute in full working order. Dr. A. H. Mitchell formerly of South Carolina was elected the first president and if my memory be correct I think he came there in the fall or winter of 1838, and probably took charge and taught in the buildings already there until the large brick buildings were ready.

This institution has been a blessing to thousands having stood and been kept in succesful operation ever since, over forty years; turning out annually more or less every year numbers who left those sacred halls with parchments showing the grade of their intellectual attainments; going forth to bless their race. The female department, I presume, have sent out as many graduates as any institution in the land. Hundreds that are now mothers can point with pride to old Summerfield as their Alma Mater. And but few of the professions or occupations could now be found among men where some one could point to Summerfield as giving them a start, if not

141

in completing their literary attainments. But the best of all, how many
hundreds can point to this spot as being the sacred place of their conversion to God and the starting point of a religious life and which in many
instances have ended in a happy death.

It is with gratitude to God that I now record the fact that such
were my condition then in life, financially, as to enable me to patronize
this noble institution, in which my three daughters now living and one of
my step-daughters were educated; and where such religious impressions were
produced upon their minds which led them to adopt a moral and religious
course through life, as the basis of all true happiness and usefulness
and which to me now is a source of exquisite comfort to know that these
influences are not lost upon their growing and rising posterity. In addition to these, two of my sons Willie and Robert had the advantage of this
institution for one session. Where they done well and left it carrying
with them a good name for morality, industry, obedience to order and
advancement in their studies. But the best of all was that in addition
to religious impressions, love of the church and reverence for God, which
had been made upon their minds previously were now under the fostering care
of pious preceptors and the many religious influences under which they were
here placed not only strengthened those impressions, but finally culminated
in their love for and connection with the church of their parents. But
more on this subject hereafter.

Being now engaged in farming and having a considerable interest to
look after at the end of that year I asked and obtained of the Conference
which convened at Tuscaloosa, Alabama January 1st, 1840 a location and
ended my itinerant course; having from that time to the present sustained
to the church, the relation of Local Elder.

- Incidents and Labours of 1840 -

My time was now employed in attending through the week to the business
of my farm and settling up the estate of my wife's first husband, she being
the executrix of his will, by virtue of our marriage I became associated in
that capacity with her. And although was a business in which I had no
experience, yet it had been managed so prudently and correctly by my wife's
uncle David Wardlaw, acting as agent for her, who now transferred it all
into my hands very much against my will, that in assuming this position I
found the way so well marked out that I got on with the business much more
easily and satisfactorly than I had expected and finally after having to

defend in Chancery Court a long litigated law suit which we gained and
having paid up all the indebtedness I made a final settlement without having
to sell any property which had been bequeathed in the will and saving to
the children near two thousand dollars over and above the legacies left
them in the will and which I finally paid over to them and received from
them the assurance of satisfaction with the management of their fathers
estate.

– My First Sons Birth –

This occured on the 14th of January of this year and was named by
my wife's Uncle for himself "David Wardlaw", who at the time of naming him,
was sick and not expecting to live desired of us both who were then with
him to let him give our boy a name to which we consented. He, at the time
had me engaged writing his will, in it he bequeathed to all his nephews who
had been named after him a certain legacy, besides dividing the balance
of his estate among his relatives. And in this distribution left to our
son one thousand dollars, besides a certain portion to my wife and her
children separately. After the will was written he told me to fold it
up and put it in a certain dresser and when company came in he would sign
it. He continued to linger and although I was with him frequently yet
feeling a delicacy and knowing him to be a very correct and prompt man in
his business affairs, believing he had signed and fixed up his will, as he
had been up and able to go about and attend to other business, never asked
him about it and after he died I found the document in the same condition
as I had left it not signed except it showed some signs of having been
handled by him. Thus was every legatee named in that will deprived of
realizing any thing by it. He had no family, had lived a bachelor, amassed
a fine property and at his death or afterwards scattered to the four winds.

– His Death –

This took place, if my recollection be correct, in the spring or
early in the summer of that year and his remains were interred in the grave
yard at Fellowship Church, Mount-Moriah, Wilcox County, Alabama.

It now became necessary in the absence of a will that his estate be
put into the hands of an administrator for final adjustment and settlement.
I corresponded with some of his relatives, particularly my wife's father,
at Abbeville, South Carolina who insisted that I should become administrator
and take it in charge at once. The responsibility danger and labour of such
a charge was so great that I hesitated for some time, but it being the wish

143

of my wife and her relatives besides the advice of some of my intimate
friends, vis: John McReynolds, Willie Williams, Thomas Armstrong, and
others, several of whom voluntarily offered to be my bondsmen; I consented
and took the business in hand.

The estate was large, consisting in real and personal property and
a considerable amount in money loaned at sixteen percent. And its
distribution had to be divided between his brothers and sisters, several
of whom were dead and left large families of children; and some of these
dead leaving children as their representatives so on ascertaining the
exact number of distributees, I found it amounted to thirty six and
scattered over five (if no more) states from South Carolina to Texas.

(Copied from original written by Rev. A. C. Ramsey)

(Rev. A. C. Ramsey died at Forest Home, Butler County, Alabama,
  January 23, 1891.   Anson West)

146

147

148

www.ingramcontent.com/pod-product-compliance
Lightning Source LLC
Chambersburg PA
CBHW020015030726
47500CB00002B/600